Leah T. Williams

Neither Out Far
Nor In Deep

PERIGON PUBLISHING LLC
ATLANTA, GA

I0544375

NEITHER OUT FAR NOR IN DEEP

First edition. January 24, 2023.

Copyright © 2023 Leah T. Williams.

ISBN: 978-1962776035

Written by Leah T. Williams.

CHAPTER 1

His office was bland, just a small room with nothing on the walls. No windows. No degrees. No pictures of family. Not even a flag from the school he went to. Nothing. Just a room with a peeling desk and a chair on each side. Their cushions looked as though they were once a vibrant blue before they came here to die. He sat on the desk with one foot planted on the ground and the other in the chair.

"Sit!" He motioned for me to sit in the empty chair. Didn't he know that tables weren't for sitting and chairs weren't for feet? He was an animal, this guy. Nothing like Dean Fidge, the tenth-grade dean. She talked to me the whole way to her office, and she'd never sneak up on me the way this guy always did. I heard her coming a mile away like she was making an announcement or something. I always saw her around this area even though this was mostly the eleventh-grade building. Not sure if she patrolled the area but whenever I saw her, she spoke to me. She didn't talk to me in a scolding way either, like she wanted to be Ma or somebody. She talked to me like she could be one of my boys, if I had any. I liked her. She was cool. At least her room reminded me of when I passed by the Bath and Body Works. Her room smelled like how one of those Disney movies probably smelled, the one with a princess, sweet. And I at least knew she was a Florida Gator fan cause it was nothing but Gator gear plastered all over her walls and pictures of her with people laughing, one with her in a white long dress with some dude, and another one with her in the middle of two old people. It just smelled like old locker room in here, before the janitor came to clean up, sweaty and musky. I wished I could open a window.

"So, Kadeem," Dean Monti began. The dean of students, at least for my grade, he usually kept his walkie-talkie on silent so he could startle me from behind. Kind of creepy. With all the other deans shouting in their walkie-talkie was a form of warning, enough of a warning to know that I'd better pretend to do something else, something I wouldn't actually get in trouble for.

"So, Mr. Monti," I responded with the same dean-ish attitude. I wanted to put my feet on the desk, interlace my fingers behind my head and lean back, but that would be taking it too far, even for me. Instead, I sat in the chair and waited for my scolding.

"So, why are we here?"

"You work here sir, and me?" I knew this wasn't the answer he wanted but why not play this game he loved so much? "I just go to school here."

"You know what I mean, Kadeem! Why are you in my office?"

"You told me to come to your office, practically dragged me. Since you are the adult, I didn't think that I had much of a choice."

He put down his other leg and stood. He was a tall dude. Big too, like he used to play football or something or maybe wrestle. His full beard almost covered his lips. Only a stare could define their movement. I wasn't gonna be staring in no man's face like that though.

I sat up, no longer relaxed. I braced myself for what was to come. I hated having my back to the door. I'd been handcuffed before, not arrested, but, handcuffed. I was in this very room when it happened, talking to Dean Monti. And just when I thought I was gonna get suspended again, the school's resource officer came in, dragged me out of my seat, pushed me up against the wall, and jammed on the cuffs. I had to wait in that office with my wrists bound together, behind my back, until Ma came to pick me up. My wrists were bruised by the time they took them off. So, yeah, I braced myself. I relaxed a little but not enough to slouch in the chair cause it wasn't gonna happen again. He opened his desk and pulled out a long pink paper and a pen.

"Kadeem, you know I hate doing this."

"Then don't."

"I'm going to have to." He leaned over the paper and started writing. I hadn't noticed before but he was left handed. He wrote almost using his entire left shoulder to scribble whatever he was scribbling. He looked like he was hiding his work from someone who would copy it.

"Do what you have to," I shrugged.

"This is the third time this month I've had to suspend you. And don't think that the other young man is going to get out of it either." His voice boomed louder and deeper with each word. "Aren't you sick of being in here?"

"Yeah." I say. I was sick of being in here. But this time it was for a good reason. I was defending myself and I said that, too, hoping that I could escape punishment. I really was defending myself. I was just walking in the hallway. Yeah, the bell rang. Yeah, I wasn't supposed to be there but dude wasn't supposed to be there either. He just pushed me like there was no more space in the hallway.

Wide-ass hallway with plenty of squares on the floor but he just had to invade my square. Of course, I had to defend myself because dudes be thinking cause I'm not as big as them, they gonna just disrespect me in all kinds of ways. Naw, it's not gonna happen. I told dean Monti all of this and it looked like he was listening. He looked like he was agreeing with me cause he was shaking his head as I spoke, but he still wrote on his long pink paper.

"These things are not just for fighting." He held up his hands already balled up into fists, one of his bigger than my two put together. "You have got to stop using them to ruin your life."

"Here we go." I rolled my eyes and slouched low in my seat, setting myself up for the usual lecture.

"Each time I suspend you, what happens?"

"I miss school."

"What happens when you miss school?"

"I miss out on a free education." We've been here before so I repeated exactly what we've said before.

"So, I am going to have to suspend you - again. We do not tolerate any type of violence on our campus. However, since you have stated that you were not the aggressor, you will only be suspended for five days."

"Five days?" I shouted.

"Yes, five days, Kadeem. I hate to do this but I'm going to have to. It seems like this is the only way you're going to learn."

"Learn?" I mumbled.

"Yes, son." He put the pen down and looked directly at me. "I know that you can check yourself out of school but I'm still going to have to call your mother to let her know how you've behaved here today."

"Call her then! And thanks for the pep talk." I hung my book bag from one shoulder and walked out. The school's resource officer was outside the dean's office draining the last sip of his venti Frappuccino cup. I wanted to walk faster but I was wearing socks and slides so I moved as fast as they'd let me which wasn't nearly fast enough. At the gate, the security guard nodded at me but then it looked like he was nodding at the cop, hinting to him that it was alright for me to walk through the gate for a five-day suspension that wasn't even my fault.

Once I was through the gate, I covered my ears with my Beats. I liked these ones Ma got me cause they completely covered my ears and shut everything out. They were a little expensive but it was the only gift I wanted for Christmas, plus the Nike windbreaker and the white Nike Air-force Ones. They were classics. The Air-force Ones, not the Beats. The sounds of the Beats drifted through them like nothing else mattered, nothing else existed, just me and my music. Bad thing that they didn't connect to my playstation. That's right, I'd be able to play 2K for a full week with no interruptions. Suspension wasn't going to be so bad after all.

At home, in the driveway was Ma's car. She must've caught a ride to work. She and Janine sometimes carpooled to save gas, she said, but I think it was just because Janine was my mother's only friend. She ain't got nobody else really, at least nobody I'd seen around.

I headed straight for the kitchen cause I was thirsty as hell walking from school. School wasn't far from home but any kind of walking in the hot sun made everything seem far. From the fridge, I grabbed the bottle of orange juice and pressed the entire bottle to my head. It was only a little left so I finished it. No plastic bag in the empty trash can so I shoved the empty bottle back in the refrigerator. I'd get it later.

I took the stairs two-by-two to my bedroom, my place of solace, I prayed my PlayStation remotes weren't dead.

Whoa! Ma rummaged through my room like she was looking for something.

"Ma?" I called out. "Ma!" I asked again but she searched my drawers and threw my stuff on my bed.

"I can't any more, Kadeem..."

"Can't what, Ma?" I asked her cause now she was scaring me.

"I just can't," she said again. "I've tried any and everything."

"Did something happen at work, Ma?" Man, she was really tripping, and I couldn't imagine what it could be. She was an ER nurse and all sorts of things be happening at that place. She always be looking stressed when she got home - when I do see her.

"Work?" She stopped and shouted at me. "Work? Are you serious right now?"

"Yes, Ma, did something happen at work?" I asked again quietly cause now I was thinking somebody musta died on her watch or something.

"Kadeem, obviously you're not getting it."

"Getting what, Ma?" And I do get it. But, hey, this time it wasn't even my fault. I was only defending myself. This one really couldn't be avoided. I mean, I couldn't imagine having a child who was always getting in trouble so I was honestly trying to keep my head down.

"You don't get it." She shook her head and looked at me briefly, just enough for me to see her puffy eyes and runny nose. She pulled my rolling duffle bag from under my bed and started cramming what was on the bed into the duffle bag. This was my cruise bag -

the bag I used when we went on cruises. This was not Ma's cruise behavior though.

As Ma crammed the clothes in the bag, I started pulling them out and pushing them back in my drawers.

"Kadeem!" She roared. I'd only heard my mother this loud when she was mad and she'd been mad at me a whole lot lately. I knew this voice though. I was taller than her but still scared whenever she used that voice. I immediately stopped taking my clothes from my bag because everything seemed to stop in midair like when you heard that scary music just before someone was about to be killed in a movie. Like you knew something bad was about to happen, but you just didn't know when and how.

Time started and Ma was stuffing clothes in my bag in no particular order again. She wasn't looking to match a shirt with pants or nothing. The bag became bigger and bigger as she tried to push more and more of my clothes in the bag that was obviously running out of room. I wanted to tell her that the bag couldn't hold anything else, that if she tried to shove one more thing in the bag, she wouldn't be able to close it. Tears streamed down her face. She mumbled words I couldn't understand. There was no way she was gonna hear what I had to say even if it made sense. She grunted as she tried to zip the bag.

"Ma, lemme help!"

She shoved me from the bag and sat on it. The zipper still didn't budge. She pulled a shirt from the bag, then another, then another, when she realized it wasn't closing. She finally got it shut and then bent over and dragged the bag then stopped, then dragged it and stopped until she got to the top of the stairs. She kicked the bag and it muddled down the stairs and landed with a thud at the bottom.

"Let's go!" She shouted.

"Where, Ma?" I asked. "Where are we going?"

"I don't have time for this, Kadeem! GET YOUR ASS IN THE CAR!"

Whenever she cursed, I knew she was serious and really really mad so I got in the car. She got in too, slammed the car door and started driving.

"Where we going, Ma?" I asked again cause this wasn't making no sense.

She didn't answer. We rode in deafening silence. Not even the radio. Straight up highway 436 we passed the new Chipotle, the new Starbucks, and Mcdonald's. She heard the rumble of my stomach and didn't even stop. In fact, she didn't even ask if I was hungry when I got home. She musta been really really mad.

She drove into the parking section of terminal B of the airport.

"Ma!" I called. "Seriously. Where we going?" My voiced cracked.

Still no answer.

She parked on the fourth floor, section F. I tried to remember that cause Ma never would.

She got out, slammed her door and raced around to my side. Immediately, my door was opened and she was tugging on my hoodie.

"Let's go, Kadeem!" She shouted.

I hated when people shouted at me, especially Ma!

I followed her and the duffle bag. I still wasn't going to help her cause she still wasn't telling me where we were going. In the elevator, still silence from her. She punched the *Tunnel* button and we sank in silence. Good thing no one else was in the elevator to stare cause we stood in the elevator, Ma in her scrubs and her overstuffed duffle bag and me in my jeans, oversized hoodie, slides, and socks, looking like we didn't belong.

Ma walked up to the ticket counter and mumbled something to the lady. There were few people in the airport. It may have been this slow because it was in the middle of the day. Maybe they were all in school where I was supposed to be or at work where Ma was supposed to be.

"Let's go!" Ma ordered.

I followed her and with my shoes, headphones, and cellphones in the bin, we breezed through TSA. I still didn't know where we were going and why.

In the train towards the departure gate and she was still silent. Her silence was worse than her shouting and I really hated her shouting but, at that moment I would've preferred it. At gate 44 we didn't wait long until the announcement, "WE ARE NOW BOARDING FLIGHT 661 FROM ORLANDO TO MIAMI."

"Ma, what we going to Miami for?"

Silence.

"Somebody die?"

Silence.

Her hand was empty cause she checked the duffle bag a while back. Just a small bag draped over her shoulder.

We boarded and were not seated together. Ma sat several seats behind me and I sat by myself. The plane was empty, emptier than the airport if that was possible. It was just us, a few more passengers, and the people who worked on the plane. We've only taken a plane once to Miami to take a cruise. All the other times we went on cruises, Ma drove from Orlando to Miami or from Orlando to Tampa, or from Orlando to Port Canaveral. Any other time we took a plane from Orlando to Miami was when Ma was taking us back to her hometown for vacation. But none of us was on vacation time. Ma was still in her scrubs and school was still in for me, suspended or not.

I felt a hard lash on my shoulder. It was Ma. I must've fallen asleep. We left the plane and I followed her. She walked further into the airport and she passed a TGIFridays, the restaurant. That was our place. That was where me and a Ma went out to eat, just me and her. And my stomach still rumbled but Ma sped pass our place like I didn't usually order a full rack of BBQ ribs and Ma a cheeseburger with no onions. But she didn't stop and we walked by Friday's like it wasn't what we did, like it didn't even exist.

I heard the announcement before we even got there and Ma got a chance to sit. They were already boarding. "ALL PASSENGERS ON FLIGHT 227 WITH FULL SERVICE FROM MIAMI TO ST. KITTS IS NOW BOARDING."

And then it hit me, we were going to St. Kitts. But why, I didn't know.

CHAPTER 2

The plane's motion jerked me awake. Clapping broke out as though the pilot did something good. I mean, I guess he did. We weren't dead. Before the plane came to a full stop, people were already getting up to get their things from the overhead bins making the cylinder smaller than it actually was. I didn't have my duffel. Ma didn't have my duffel. So, we didn't move.

Ma was still upset. She rolled her eyes and shook her head when she looked at me. She was only a seat behind me again and she was watching me like, if it was legal, she'd kill me for real real.

We waited for our turn to stand. We were way in the back - 38A and 39F - so that meant that we were exiting through the back of the plane. Not that I travelled a lot but this was so different from Orlando, even Miami. We've never exited a plane in the States from the rear. At the aircraft's door, Ma stopped for a moment, inhaled, sighed and her entire body relaxed. It really did smell better here without cars backfiring. Ma told me a story once about when I was younger, and we were flying into St. Kitts. She said it wasn't my first time flying in but it must've been the first time when I was able to talk. She said I was about three and she used to always give me the window seat so that I could see the island as we landed, an experience that she enjoyed herself. She said as we were getting closer to the ground, I blurted out "Ain't no cars here Ma." She said she was so embarrassed that I said that because I acted like her country wasn't modern enough to have cars. I wondered if she remembered.

She continued down the stairs and I followed. We walked from the runway to the building that was encased in large glass windows like a fish bowl with people inside. Red, bold letters spelling Robert L Bradshaw International Airport were sprawled across the building where anyone could see, even in the night. Unlike Orlando, there wasn't anything that the plane could attach itself to in order to get us directly into the building. We had to walk on that pavement.

The heat hit my face instantly reminded me that most buildings on the island didn't have AC. Did houses have AC? What were we doing here? I wanted to ask. But I didn't dare say a thing. I followed Ma up the stairs to Customs cause here she could hit me and nobody gonna say nothing to her like they would in Orlando. Home, somebody would call the police real quick if she ever hit me. She's told me that before, threatened me, I guessed. But the truth was that she ain't never really hit me, not for real real anyway.

"Ma, is Grandad okay?" I asked because I thought that was the only family she had left here and I couldn't imagine any other reason why we'd fly out like we were running from the Mafia or something. This really would be a good place for witness protection. It was so small, you'd see anyone coming in from the time they stepped off the plane, either from the back or the front of the plane. Home, everybody looked different anyway so we kinda fit in. Here? It was obvious who were natives and who weren't. Clearly, the people who were sweating like they'd just ran a marathon, including me and Ma, were not natives. Our bodies were not used to this heat and it was showing. For the natives, the heat didn't seem to be an issue. They weren't suffering the way we were. Ma still didn't answer me but I followed her anyway. She walked up the stairs from the runway with the rest of the passengers. I followed silently.

Two different lines in the airport announced "Welcome Vistors" and "Welcome Home, Natives." Ma went in the "Welcome Home, Natives" line like she actually lived here. She hadn't lived here since she was a teenager as far as I knew but every time we visited, she went in that same line, refusing to acknowledge that this was in fact no longer her home. I followed her anyway. Even though my passport was green and was stamped "born in the United States of America," I followed her because I still didn't know what was going on. It was dark outside but the large room was lit up like the sun was still out.

It was our turn next and Ma moved to the glass window. That was another thing about the *Native* line; it seemed to move more quickly than the other line. The woman behind a glass partition didn't look up. "How long were you out?" She asked while she shuffled her papers. Her accent was deep, the same way Ma sounded when she was mad.

"Just a couple of weeks," Ma lied.

The lady looked up. Maybe Ma's accent wasn't as deep as hers after all.

"Your address?" she asked suspiciously.

"Upper Lodge Project," Ma said confidently.

"Welcome home!" The lady begrudgingly said and let us by.

I followed Ma down the stairs to Luggage - well, my rolling duffle bag anyway. The large ceiling fans didn't provide enough breeze to lift my sticky t-shirt from my body. I had to remove my hoodie and tie it around my waist or I was going to die of a heatstroke. Ma fanned herself with her hand. The airport was as I remembered: three carousels, only one moved, though empty, but, I guessed ready to spit out my bag. People already lined up by the door. Guys in uniforms and brown hard hats ran up to us and asked to help with our bags. We only had one bag so bruh wasn't gonna get a dime from Ma. Surprisingly, Ma pointed at the duffle bag and the guy dragged it off of the carousel and placed it on his cart thing. I ain't never seen her do that - pay somebody to help her.

"How many more?" He asked. He looked like he was about my age, 17. I wondered how much money he made for doing this.

"That's it," Ma said.

"Ma," I said, "I could handle that one bag." She rolled her eyes and shook her head all in the same motion. The baggage dude seemed to sense that me and Ma were warring.

We waited in another line, different from the one upstairs. People were searching your bags, for what, I didn't know. I thought they already did that in the airport in Orlando. It was our turn and baggage dude lifted my duffle off the ground and onto the metal flat table.

"Open it!" The man ordered. Like an official, he wore a collared white shirt and black stiffly ironed pants, what Custom's officers wore. Ma unzipped the bag and with his stick, he dug through the bag. "Did you bring anything for anyone?" he asked.

"No," Ma replied.

"Where is his bag?" He lifted his head in my direction.

"We are sharing a bag," Ma said confidently. The man looked suspiciously at Ma cause he knew he didn't see anything in that bag that could possibly be mistaken as something that belonged to Ma. He opened his mouth as though he was about to say something else but decided otherwise. He zipped up the bag. The bag dude took it and we left the hot room to the outside where the heat seemed to have risen to another degree or ten.

Taxis, taxi drivers and their buses lined up in front of the airport ready to take people elsewhere. Surely Ma had someone picking us up but, no, because she looked out into the sea of taxi drivers as if she was trying to figure out which one to take.

"Where you want this bag, Miss?" The bagger dude asked impatiently. I guessed time was money so he likely wanted to head back inside for another customer's bags.

"I need a taxi!" Ma said. No one was picking us up because probably no one knew we were there. Shoot, I didn't even know.

Bagger Dude dragged the bag to a taxi and Ma followed him so I followed Ma. Bagger Dude threw the bag in the bus and I was glad there were no glasses in the bag cause they'd all be broken. Ma tipped him. He said thank you and hustled back into that room for someone else's bags. Ma said something to the taxi driver so low that I couldn't even hear her. Ma jumped in, so I did too. We rode in silence exiting the airport. Unlike Orlando, it was one lane in and one lane out. There was no multi-level parking garage like in Orlando, no side A or side B, just one way in and one way out. The driver swung the bus carelessly around the roundabout and I was reminded of the reasons why I hated riding in vehicles here. Not only did they drive on the wrong side of the road but the driver was also on the wrong side of the vehicle. It felt so awkward seeing him where the passenger really should be.

"You here on vacation?" the driver asked.

"No," Ma responded, "I live here." No, she didn't live here. She just didn't like giving people more information than they needed. The driver glanced suspiciously in his rearview mirror but he didn't ask any more questions cause the look on Ma's face told everybody that she didn't want to talk. I knew better. I knew not to ask any questions. I knew not to say anything.

The road narrowed which made the lane we were in seem too narrow for even this bus. Even so, vehicles whizzed by in the other direction. Other vehicles passed by us, narrowly escaping the oncoming lights to do so. I didn't have my licenses yet but I was pretty sure you couldn't cross double lines to pass a vehicle. Were the driving rules different here? The driver continued through these near-death experiences as though our lives didn't matter, or his. At each corner, both me and Ma held on to our seats to keep from falling. It must have been legal to speed here cause by now, a police officer or state trooper would've stopped this speeding taxi already. But, nothing. No sirens. Not one police officer was visible.

Though it was night, the streets were still busy. There were several people on the streets as we passed by. Some leaned against the walls of buildings while others just sat on the side of the street sipping from glass bottles. Clearly, they were hanging out and no one was bothering them and telling them that they were loitering. Lights were still shining through the windows of some of the houses and shadows moved about in them. I guessed everyone didn't go to bed early. The driver turned his left blinker on and waited for an upcoming car. The car passed and our driver turned up a steep hill where only a few houses were lit up. Guess the other people knew that it was time to go to sleep. It was already after midnight according to my phone which meant that it was after eleven here. Something that I knew Ma paid attention to when she called Grandad. There were times when she'd remind me that St. Kitts didn't have day light savings time. Time was time here, she'd say, no need to change it. My phone was not going to update to their time until I got WiFi.

Maybe something was wrong with Grandad. It's not like I knew him that well but being my mom's only family left, I knew she'd be devastated if he was sick or something. She tapped her fingers on the seat like they were little men marching to nowhere. She sucked in deep breaths then let them out again like she was trying to keep from blowing up or reacting in a way that she didn't want to, something she taught me to do before I made a bad decision. I had never actually tried it though. It looked like it was working for her cause she hadn't strangled me yet. Over and over her fingers loudly marched in place on the seat and she breathed in an out. I looked at her from the side, careful not to stare because that was not going to do me any good. I really hoped Grandad was okay.

"Which house, Miss?" The driver asked.

"The green one on the top of the hill," Ma responded. She pointed ahead to an unlit house. "The one on the right," She continued.

The driver didn't stop despite her instructions. She didn't speak, so, I didn't either. The driver turned around at the top of the hill so that his bus faced the direction we came from. As Ma opened the door, I tried to help her but she shrugged me off. "*Struggle then.*" I wanted to say but I didn't dare. Ma dragged the bag out of the taxi. The driver made no attempt to leave his wrong driver's side seat to help. He just sat there as though his job was finished.

I stood taller than the bright green wall fence that surrounded the house, but the iron bars towered over me. The lights were off inside the house as though no one was expecting us. I looked at Ma, she was still practicing her breathing exercises, but slower than before. It was pitch dark, a kind of dark that didn't seem safe in any kind of movie. Plus, the driver didn't even wait for us to get inside before he bolted. Though it was night, the grass shone.

"Daddy!" Ma yelled out and a dog barked loudly. Once that dog started, it was like an alarm for the others because barks and howling started to come from everywhere. I just hoped that there wasn't a dog inside the yard that we were going in to.

"Ma," I said. "Maybe he's not home."

She ignored me and continued to yell. "Daaaahdaaay." She screamed, lengthening the sound of *daddy*. It was like when she called me from her bedroom to bring her something and added all these eee's to my name, *Kadeeeeeem*. She wouldn't stop calling me until I stood in front of her. I didn't know if she thought that made it louder or what but a light came on outside. The light revealed two steps that lead up to the door. The door slowly opened and an older Grandad than I remembered peaked out.

"Gwendolyn?" he asked. Only Grandad called Ma by her full name like that. Everyone else called her Gwen.

"Yes, Daddy," Ma responded. "It's me, me and Kadeem."

CHAPTER 3

Grandad was barefoot out the door and down the two steps. His feet sunk in the grass as he came closer to us. It must've rained earlier cause his footsteps sounded kind of soggy. He fiddled with the lock on the gate and it made a clanging noise on the iron gate as Grandad pulled it off.

"Gwendolyn?" Grandad asked as though to make sure she was who he indeed saw. "Is wa you doing out ya gyal?" He looked at Ma, then me. "You tell me you was coming?"

"No," Ma said. "I just decided to-"

"You just decide to wa?" Grandad grabbed the bag and ushered Ma into the house. He left me there to fend for myself, but I followed them anyway cause I wasn't gonna stay outside with all the dogs barking and howling. "You just decided to get on a plane and come ya?"

"Yes, Daddy," Ma said.

We stood in a room that looked like it was both the kitchen and the living area. Somehow everything seemed so much smaller than I last remembered. Or, maybe I was smaller and everything seemed bigger. Either way, the love seat, couch, and single seater encircled a table with a glass top. Pictures crowded each other on the glass top. One with me in my YMCA uniform with a soccer ball. One with me in my YMCA uniform playing basketball. One with me in my YMCA uniform playing flag football. I was little though. None of me now. Ma musta stop sending pictures or maybe I stopped taking them. Man, I used to play a lot of sports when I was little. There was one with Ma in her cap and gown maybe when she graduated nursing school. I was little then, not in that picture but Ma had that same picture, except I was holding her graduating cap. No space allowed me to get to any of the seats, so I just stood. I would have had to step over the arm of a love seat and the single seat in order to actually sit. I remained, cause I still didn't know how pissed Ma was.

"You travel in your wuk clothes? Wat really goin' on, Gwendolyn?" Grandad's voice was firm as if he expected a real answer and immediately.

"Daddy, I can't deal with Kadeem anymore." Ma started to cry and immediately I started to look for ways to disappear. Right then I wished that the floor would swallow me up so that I wouldn't have to see her crying. I hated when she did that, especially when it was because it was over something I did or she thought I did.

"Gyal, hush you mout'!" Grandad demanded. Then he looked at me. "Go in dat room, Kadeem." He pointed to the door on the left. He told Ma to sit down at a table in the kitchen area. I left a crack in the door so that I could hear their voices. Shoot, I should be in the room if they were talking about me; I heard Ma's sobs, but she was trying to control them, almost like she was trying to stop. Grandad didn't say anything.

"Daddy, he got suspended again."
Silence.
"I don't know what else to do,"
Silence.

"I just thought, maybe -" Ma sobbed again. "I just don't know, Daddy. I don't know what to do."

Silence.

"The only thing he does at school is get in trouble."

Silence.

"I don't even want to answer the phone anymore from the school because I know, Daddy-" She blew her nose, a long and messy sound like she was having a real nasty cry, like she been waiting to release them since we been flying.

Silence.

"I just know they are calling me to get Kadeem because of another fight."

Silence.

"He's always fighting, daddy." She sobbed, "Always."

Silence.

"I don't even know what this last fight was about. I just know that he was fighting," Ma said. Her disappointed made me want to go out and explain that, yeah, I had been fighting a lot but this one time, it really wasn't my fault. I really couldn't avoid it. But like the Dean, I knew she wasn't going to listen. She didn't want to. All those other times I fought, this is the one I really couldn't avoid. I wondered if Grandad could even understand. At this point, I didn't even think anyone could. Why even try?

I looked around the room cause I was tired. I was sure it was tomorrow in Orlando and I had already had such a long day. Exhausted, I looked at my phone, one bar, almost dead, still on airplane mode. I dared not take it off airplane mode cause if there was any reason Ma would really kill me besides this last suspension, it would be to run up her AT&T bill. This place was not one of the fifty states or territories so Ma would definitely be charged roaming fees. I planned to ask Grandad for the WIFI password and use WIFI til we left. I looked around the room, a single full-sized bed waited in the middle of the room with a large cherrywood chest of drawers next to it, very similar to my room in Orlando. I had one window though and that faced our neighbor's wall cause the houses were so close to each other, not exactly a good view. Grandad had two windows in this room. One was facing the street and the other was facing the neighbor's house but several tall trees blocked the full sight of the house. Both louvres of the windows were open, letting in a slight breeze, slowly and barely lifting the thin blue curtains. It was still hot in here. I'd never leave my window open in Orlando, there were too many chances of people breaking in or worse, critters. A fan hung from the ceiling, I turned it on. The light came on with it so I pulled the string to turn the lights off but kept the fan on. It sounded like they had finished talking about me anyway so I slid my slides off, took off my t-shirt and laid down in the bed, directly under the fan.

A sound of a rooster outside of the window woke me, so loud as if it was under the bed I slept in, but I knew it was not. The sun wasn't even up yet. I looked at my phone, still one bar. I hoped to God Ma remembered to pack the chargers when she was cramming my duffel. If not, hopefully, I could use Grandad's charger til we left. I walked out the room and the door leading to the backyard was wide open. Ma was not there. She must have been in the other bedroom. I didn't wake her because I knew she was tired. She really needed rest. This get away was going to be good for the both of us. Grandad was outside, barefoot, taking shirts from a bucket, squeezing them so that water drained out of them, and hanging them on the clothesline that led from the fence to a pole in the middle of the yard. I cleared my throat so that I didn't startle him. I sure didn't want to be blamed for one more thing, especially giving an old man a heart attack.

"I tink you mean to say good mawning!" Grandad said and he continued to pin clothes on the line. On several lines, he pinned up all sorts of clothes, faster and faster. There was just a light from the shed in the back of the yard.

"Good morning, Grandad!" I responded quickly.

"Good mawning, Kadeem," like we did this every morning. "Go get ready!" He commanded. I wanted to ask *for what*, cause I didn't have no school, and I didn't have no job, so get ready for what? But I didn't say nothing and just did what Grandad said. The last thing I wanted was to upset him too. I needed at least one person on my side before we went back home.

I wheeled my duffle into the room I slept in. Great! Just like I thought, nothing matched nothing. I wished Ma told me what she was doing so I could actually help pack my own clothes. I just shook my head and pulled out a gray t-shirt and some Nike joggers. Man, it was way too hot to wear joggers and it was gonna be even hotter later. I put them on any way and finished up with my slides and socks from last night. I walked out and found that Grandad was already fully dressed. How did he move this fast? He was wearing a short sleeve collared blue shirt, khaki pants and wide brim straw hat, and Jesus sandals, the ones with his toes out. The ones where Jesus took all his pictures in. Jesus don't never be wearing no Nikes. His shirt was neatly tucked into his pants with a belt that looked like it was the only thing keeping the pants up on his waist. I wanted to tell him that those pants were too big, but I didn't say anything cause, I didn't want him to think I was trying to disrespect him; besides, it was none of my business what he wore, and, I was hungry.

The scent of bread filled my nostrils, like when you passed by Panera Bread early in the morning and the strong scent forced you to stop and buy a bagel. This was like that but instead, right in front of me. There was a loaf of bread on the kitchen table but bread and what? Usually when we visited, Ma brought a suitcase with groceries. Mac and cheese, Chef Boyardee, cereal, Pop Tarts, Doritos. Stuff was too expensive here but she brought the things I liked so I could have enough to eat. I didn't see her pack nothing like that so I guessed she was gonna buy my cereal from the store here.

I followed Grandad out the back door that lead from the kitchen. Two vehicles in the yard were parked next to the house. There was a large white gate, larger than the one we came through last night. This gate must've been the one that the vehicles used. Grandad clambered into the brown van, in the driver's side that should really be the passenger's side if we were in Orlando. Why he couldn't pick us up, I didn't know. I wasn't sure where we were going and why we were taking such a big vehicle but he didn't seem the type of man that I should disobey or even question. Ma probably still slept. I jumped in the front of the bus and put on my seatbelt for a bumpy ride.

Grandad backed out of the yard. "Close de gate!" he commanded.

"You don't have a thingy?"

"No." Grandad answered. "I don't have a ting-ee."

"Ok!" I submitted, took off my seatbelt, jumped out the van. I pulled the gate like I was playing tug of war against the wall. The gate was heavier than it looked. Once back in the van, Grandad drove off down the hill. We rode through the neighborhood, every house a different bright color and lots of people moving about, doing their own thing. Eventually, we ended out on the main road where even more people were waiting for transportation. Even school children clustered on the sides of the road waited for a ride. Here, they wore uniforms. Poor things didn't even get to wear what they wanted to school. They had to dress like robots, everybody looked the same every day. We passed rows and rows of tall plants. They couldn't be grass because they were taller and they had brownish, rods on top. After the last patch of rod grass, Grandad turned onto a street filled with more teenagers that wore the same uniform as the kids before.

"Grandad?" I asked. "Where are we going?"

"To hell if we no pray," he quipped. Not even a real answer, not to what I asked anyway. I wasn't sure why he wasn't answering my questions but I didn't like it. It was annoying as hell and disrespectful. He made me feel like I didn't even exist. Like I was talking to myself. I started to get angry but I decided to ignore that feeling I was getting that usually got me into trouble.

He parked the van and jumped out. I followed him. There was a walled fence around several buildings and a sign with a green banner that announced *Crayon High School*. I grinned cause that was a stupid name for a high school.

"Grandad, why we here?"

Silence.

I followed him to the front office. He opened the door and walked in like he had been there before. Maybe he had. Ma did go to school on this island. Maybe this was the school she attended. All the kids were in some sort of formation looking towards a stage. I could see them from the window of the office. There were a few students on the stage speaking but I couldn't make out their words. In an assembly or something, every student wore a uniform, the boys in long khaki pants or shorts, but both boys and girls in brown shirts. Some of the girls wore green skirts, and some green jumpers. Why did Grandad bring me here? I was starting not to like it.

Grandad went further behind a counter and through a hallway. I stood outside of the office until he returned. I felt very out of place with my socks and slides. I pulled my joggers up off my butt to hide my underwear cause I didn't want to draw any additional attention to myself. I was sure everybody else knew that I didn't belong there. As soon as I pulled up my joggers, Grandad returned with a man dressed in a full suit and tie. I was sure he was burning up because I was burning up in just my t-shirt and joggers. But he was not sweating.

"Here's your schedule, young man." The man offered me a piece of paper. No way that was what he said it was. A schedule? For what? For who? I got my own school. I was just here til Ma came to her senses. "We leaving soon, sir," I wanted to say.

"Naw," I said. "I'm good." And I didn't extend my hand. I didn't look at this man in his suit that he must have been hot in. Instead, I looked at Grandad like he was crazy. No way Ma was going for this. Was she moving here? Was this where we were gonna live now? No way. I wasn't going for this. If this was one of her scare tactics, it was working for sure. I was ready to head back to Orlando. Ready to be on the straight and narrow. Ready to stay out of every fight, including the ones I couldn't avoid.

CHAPTER 4

Grandad barely stopped the van before I jumped out, ran inside and searched for Ma.

"Maaaaa!" I shouted, lengthening her name like she does mine. Silence.

She wasn't laying on the couch in the one room kitchen and living room. She wasn't sitting around the small wooden table either. I walked into the room that I slept in. The bed was made, my bag neatly zipped and tucked away between the tall chest of drawers and the bed. The door to the small bathroom that separated both bedrooms was open. She wasn't there. I hesitated before I opened Grandad's door but I was desperate. It creaked. I peeked in because I didn't want to just disrespect the man's house by walking in to his private space like I had every right to. I didn't. I tried not to do things to people that I didn't like done to me. This was one of them - invading my private space. Ma always knocked before she came into my room except when she was mad. And she was mad a lot lately.

"Is wa you lookin' fa?" Grandad's voice startled me. He towered over me. My braids that were sticking up in the air, barely reached his shoulders.

"Ma," I sulked. "She's not here."

"No," Grandad said matter of factly. He walked out to the kitchen side of the big room, sat in one of the chairs and removed his shoes. Even though he wore open toed shoes, their soles were still visibly damp. His feet sweat. That had to have been where I got it from cause Ma's feet didn't sweat.

"Grandad?" I asked. "Where's Ma?" I was worried and could hear the shaking in my voice just as I could feel the shaking of the words throughout my body.

"She no ya." His voice was both deep and calm. He looked around the room as though verifying that she wasn't there and there was no way that she could've been anywhere in that place he knew so well.

"Well, where is she at, Grandad?" I plead and begged for him to give me the answer I needed to hear.

"She ga-rn home, Kadeem," as though this was the normal thing for her to do. He said this like we'd been living together forever and Ma just dropped in when she could. I wanted to scream "*THIS AIN'T NORMAL*." But I didn't.

"Home?" I plead. "But," I couldn't even finish my words. "I'm still here." I choked. Just like that I felt like breaking down and crying but I wasn't about to show that I was upset, cause I wasn't. Ma was the only one I had. If only she had listened to me when I said this last suspension wasn't really my fault. It wasn't. I had to defend myself. Even she said that I had to always defend myself. Now I was being punished for doing what she told me to do. Grandad signing me up for school here wasn't a scare tactic. It was serious. My entire body felt tight and small like I couldn't do nothing even if I wanted to. I squeezed my fists as tight as I could to keep from screaming. I wanted to punch something so badly. Instead of letting Grandad and Ma getting me mad, I just walked away. I walked to the room that they sentenced me to and slammed the door so hard that the ceiling fan shook. That was it. I gave up.

HANDS ON MY SHOULDERS shook me awake. I was groggy but tried to open my eyes. If the new day had arrived, it was Saturday so no sense in me getting up. If what I thought happened last night actually happened, I definitely wasn't going to do a thing today. I just wanted to sleep til Ma came back to scoop me up. I really did learn my lesson this time. There was nothing nobody could say to me to make me fight again. The hands shook all the sleep out of me.

"Get up!" Grandad said. "Time to go!"

Was this man insane? The rooster outside my window hadn't even crowed yet. I opened my eyes one by one. The room was dark but I could feel Grandad's presence looming over me. I dragged my fingers over the wall to feel for the light. He turned it on for me and backed up. It was as though he was waiting for me to get dressed so I did. Usually when Ma called me outta bed, I knew I at least had another thirty minutes or so before I had to actually move. Grandad wasn't budging. I hauled on the clothes from the day before, t-shirt, joggers, slides, and socks. Grandad was wearing old beat-up jeans, a shirt that used to be white at some point in its life and a different broad brimmed hat from yesterday. This hat had seen better days for sure.

"I gotta brush my teeth, Grandad," I said, hoping that that would get him up off me and gimme some space. But he didn't budge.

"Fuh wa?" He said, "you naw go use dem,"

I rubbed my eyes and followed Grandad from the bedroom, through the kitchen and out the backdoor. The moon lit up the back yard like it was a big round lamp in the sky. Grandad removed the lock from the narrow iron gate, the one that we could walk through, the one we walked through when we first got there. It was obvious that he didn't ever close that lock because it was open when we got here and it was open now. Grandad walked through the gate, waited for me to walk through and put the lock back on. He headed up the hill. I hadn't realized it before but it looked like there were rows and rows of houses just like Grandad's. They were all different colors like the red houses and green hotels on a monopoly board, except there were houses that were yellow and orange too, like they didn't have a home owner's association or something. Grandad sped up. Why didn't we take one of the two vehicles that he had parked in the yard? If he wanted to go for a walk, he could've just told me. No way my socks and slides were going to make it. I followed Grandad as we started running out of houses to pass. There were occasional barks as Grandad strode ahead of me. How this man moved so quickly, puzzled me. He had to be at least a hundred. Maybe not really, but he was certainly a senior citizen. His legs were longer than mine, so he should move faster.

"Hold up, Grandad!" I yelled, but he didn't hear me cause he kept going. I walked faster to try to catch up with him but as I did, he seemed to speed up each time I closed in. The leaves from the trees dragged across my skin as the path narrowed and became skinnier. The houses shrunk in size behind us. As we trekked through the dirt path I remembered a story from youth group. I hadn't been there for a while but I remembered some the things they used to say. The story was about this man taking his son to the mountain to sacrifice him cause God asked him to. The kid didn't even know what was happening but he laid down on the rock anyway. With the knife at the son's throat, God sent a goat or something like that in the kid's place. I mean, I knew Grandad wasn't my dad, but I wasn't about to let him sacrifice me neither. The path inclined and grew steeper. My slides barely gripped the dirt floor and I kept having to pull my pants up.

The farther and farther away we moved from the houses, the colder it got. I could never imagine it being this cold on this island, but I shivered. My legs were tired but Grandad was still moving as fast he did when we first started. I stopped to take a breath because I was winded. I bent over and heard rustling in the trees. The leaves parted and I swore a pair of eyes stared back at me.

"Grandaaaaad!" I ran. Before I knew it, the old track star in me emerged and I caught up with Grandad. "Grandad!" I panted.

"We soon reach," Grandad said recognizing that I was almost out of breath. But he moved at the same pace. I forced myself to keep up with him cause I didn't want to know what was in those trees.

At a flat part of the path, we no longer climbed. The narrow path widened and revealed a lusciously massive green area. The moon sat directly over the land making it as though it was its own personal ceiling lamp. The land was separated into large squares, each green part separated by a brown dirt path. Grandad walked in and immediately knelt at one of the squares. He dug his hand into the dirt and pulled out small little bushes.

"Me no bring you up 'ere to just stand up, eh," Grandad said gruffly and his deep voice shook me out of thoughts of my pending sacrifice. "Plenty a wuk to do."

Without question, I joined him. We used to have a garden in my elementary school with tomatoes and pumpkins and carrots and peppers so this - gardening - I at least knew how to do or at least remembered. I did what Grandad did which was picked out the weeds, the things that didn't look like they belonged. I cleaned the area around the peas, the carrots, the cabbage patches while a blended scent of dirt, sweat and greens filled my nostrils. I was exhausted but I kept going cause Grandad kept going. The chill I once felt disappeared through my sweat. I felt like the boys in this book I read in middle school, *Holes*. These bad kids were sent to camp for punishment instead of juvie and they dug holes when they were there. But I wasn't bad. I wasn't no real bad kid. Once in a while stuff happened. Things I couldn't control. Ma ain't had no right having me up here picking no weeds like a juvenile delinquent. I wasn't that neither.

"It's good to do you business before de sun start doing hers," Grandad said. He got up and brushed off the dirt from his hands onto his pants, leaving the stain on top of the already dirty looking pants. Grandad had no swagger.

"Huh?" I asked.

"We not letting de sun catch us up 'ere," Grandad explained. But the sun wasn't even close to coming out, I didn't think. The moon still hung low and gave us enough light to work. I glanced about for the sun, but instead saw Grandad making his way to the bushed opening we came through, so I followed him.

It was much easier to walk down the mountain than climbing it. Dirt ruined the shine of my slides. I thought about putting them in the washer but from the looks of things Grandad didn't have a washer. Once back to Grandad's yard, I made for the kitchen door. I had to wash this filth off of me.

"Eh," Grandad said to me. "We ain't done yet, eh." He jumped in the big van and I took my place in the passenger side that really should be the driver's side in Orlando. I wanted to ask him if vehicles were made specially for this place with the drivers on the right side instead of the left. But I didn't. I didn't want to say nothing cause I was still pissed that Ma left me here, so we rode in silence.

Grandad drove through the country with ease. People slept; the road was deserted. He drove into the city, passing the big green clock that was basically in the center of town. I remembered Ma trying to give me the history of this thing. I was sure she told me how it got there and why it was so important but I also remembered not having any interest in the history of some stupid clock.

Grandad parked in the middle of two cars, something that I still couldn't do and Ma seemed as though she was tired of trying to teach me. I mean she just left me here so she wasn't on my list of people I could depend on anymore anyway, and that was already a very short list. Grandad crossed the street and walked over to the seashore. Unlike Grandad, I looked both ways between whizzing cars. Small boats lined the seashore and men dragged in their boats from the ocean onto the shore. The sun was slowly making its way pass the moon as it sprawled part of its round body atop of the ocean's bed. I stood next to Grandad as he spoke with one of the fishermen. The man gave Grandad some of his fish. Fishes? They were grouped together and dangled from a hook, eyes wide opened. Grandad handed them to me like we did this all the time. Like we came to the seashore and bought fish from random people all the time. He handed fish to me all the time. And I held on to them all the time. "Grandad, I don't want to hold these," I protested.

"Boy, de ting Dem dead," He explained.

"Yeah, but they stink,"

"Boy, grab de ting dem cause is dis we eating,"

I grabbed hold of them with the tips of my fingers and tried my best not to let them touch me. No such luck. The closer they got to me, the more pungent they became. Their scent overpowered the scent of the salty ocean. Their scent overpowered the fact that I hadn't brush my teeth yet. Their scent overpowered the dirt that I was wearing from the mountain garden. Their scent was now in charge of all scents.

I followed Grandad back to the other side of the street. I held those things but with my arm extended, away from me while Grandad's hands were completely free. By the van, he took them from me and put them in the back. I followed him into the building behind the van. It was a farmer's market, at least what looked like a farmer's market. We had those in Orlando, but here, they sold meat. Each person's section was neatly set up with large opened baskets displaying brightly colored foods. Carts with bright orange carrots, green and yellow mangoes, light green cabbage, dark green avocados, yellow squash, green soursops and breadnut, golden yellowish star apples. Fresh herbs like thyme and green onions. Yellow and green plantains next to yellow and green bananas. These were all the things that Ma has dragged me to the West side to find, then called out the name of each one as though we were in a Caribbean food museum, and she was our guide. She did it every time too like I needed to hear the names of those things every time we went. I didn't. She'd hold up the ridged fruit and say, "star apple." Then she'd pick up the green, almost round fruit with spikes and say, "soursop." She'd do this for every island originated fruit or vegetable in the store. By now I had to know their names. I was glad Grandad didn't do the same thing. Grandad walked quickly into the market, briefly looked at each section then quickly moved on to another. We just came from a garden that I was sure had all this stuff. Why were we even here? Grandad stopped to talk to some of the farmers. Grandad laughed and his entire body shook. He bought at least one thing from almost every farmer's stand so, now, we had a bunch of different vegetables and fruits, some of the same things that I just cleaned weeds from. I was glad Grandad had friends or at least people he could laugh with. He looked so at home with these people, like he really belonged here. But what about me? When would I get to go home?

CHAPTER 5

The sound of the rooster woke me. He crowed like his life depended on it. It was his job and he was gonna do his best. Saturday was so long and busy that I must've slept through the whole of Sunday. Grandad just let me too. He didn't wake me not one time, not even to eat and now I was hungry. I heard pots and pans loudly hitting each other. Maybe Ma was back to scoop me up cause I definitely learned my lesson. I wasn't gonna fight no more. I walked out to the kitchen and a man's voice was coming from the radio. No Ma. She wasn't back yet. The announcer was coming through loud and clear saying *and so and so is survived by....* He said one name after the other while this ominous music played in the background. Who'd want to listen to this first thing in the morning? Grandad. He stood next to the ironing board and pressed down on something brown and listened to all the names of the people who died and the names of their relatives.

"Grandad?" I asked. "Why you listening to this stuff?" I'm so used to Ma watching <u>Good Morning America</u> or something, if she was home in the morning. But, Grandad's television was off. In fact, since I'd been there, I didn't even ever remember seeing it on, not one time.

"Good mawning," Grandad said, ignoring my question.

"Why you listening to all these dead people names, Grandad?" I asked again.

"Is me you sleep wid last night, bwoy?" Grandad asked. I knew what he was asking me to do too. I remembered Ma used to do this very thing. She didn't answer anything I asked her until I greeted her. Once I greeted her, we could have a full conversation like she didn't just scold me for saying *Good morning* although I'd seen her the night before.

"Good morning, Grandad!" I submitted.

"You gah tu hear who dead to know who living." Grandad continued after my *good morning*. Same thing Ma did. This must've been where she got that from.

"Huh?"

"Come over here side me!" Grandad demanded. I walked over and stood next to him.

"Yes, Grandad?" He smelled like mint and mangoes. He wore long khakis and a cool floral buttoned-down shirt. His skin was smooth like he just shaved and there was no new growth. I shaved once, a long time ago, when I only had a little bit of hair. It grew out all weird like, from different parts of my face, no real pattern. So, I took one of Ma's pink razors and drug it across my face. Big mistake. Not only were there cuts all over my face when I was done, but my hair grew back all sorts of weird ways, a stranger pattern than originally. Then they fell out. Now, I just had some stragglers under my chin. But, Grandad, his face was smooth.

"You know how to iron?" he asked. He continued to iron the brown shirt.

"Not really," I said, "I mean, Ma was trying to teach me but I don't really got clothes that need ironing and when I do, Ma takes them to the cleaners."

"You mean to tell me Gwendolyn ain't teach you how to iron you clothes?" He shook his head in disappointment.

"Grandad, I don't really wear clothes that need ironing." I told him cause it was the truth. There was no real reason to iron stuff. Even my church clothes when, I did go to church, were always dry cleaned. I'd take them off, put them in the wash and I'd meet them in my closet. No ironing.

"A goin' iron dis fu you today, but tomorrow, you gah tu iron dis you-self."

"What?" I asked. "Iron what?"

"You uniform, bwoy. Day not goin' let you in de school like dat." That was when it hit me. He was ironing my school uniform. It was Monday. I'd already slept through Sunday. Ma wasn't back and this was for real.

I DIDN'T KNOW WHERE Grandad got all these things from so quickly and how he knew my size. We got in Thursday night. School visit on Friday. Ma left on Friday. Mountain visit on Saturday. I didn't know when he had time to get a uniform, but, I was now fully dressed in long khaki pants, brown belt and brown collared shirt. My shoes were brown with thick soles. The only thing I liked about these shoes were that they gave me a little height. I was just about an inch closer to Grandad's shoulders.

"You look nice, bwoy!" Grandad said to me when I walked out of the bedroom. I swear I wasn't feeling nice. I wasn't really feeling anything but confusion. I couldn't believe that this was really happening. Was I really going to a new school? In this new place? For how long? The duration of my suspension? How long? Til Ma wasn't mad no more? How long? I couldn't remember the last time I wore a belt or even shoes that were all the same color. Height or not, I didn't like the shoes so I went back in the room to find some other kicks, something that would make the fit, ya know...better. Nothing. There wasn't nothing in that duffle bag that Ma packed, no shoes, anyway. So, basically all I had was my slides and these new shoes. I walked out the bedroom again, disappointed that I couldn't change my shoes to what I really wanted. Uniform or not, I knew for a fact that I had at least five or more pairs of shoes that could make this fit better than it was.

"Why you face look so?" Grandad asked. My face was scrunched up. I guess what I was feeling was seeping out.

"I don't like this fit, Grandad," I held my arms out to show him how stupid I looked.

"Fit?" Grandad asked. "You no like how it fit?"

"Fit!" I repeated. "As in outfit. I don't like this outfit"

"You tink a pig does wuk in a dog skin?"

"Huh?"

"You goin' school," Grandad declared. "Dis is day uniform!" He pointed at my clothes. "Dis what you gah tu wear in de people dem school!" I got it now, I understood what he was saying. Ma didn't usually say these things that Grandad had been saying. Ma spoke more clearly, slowly, except when she was mad. Grandad spoke like he was speaking in riddles most of the times, when he did talk. So, essentially, he was saying that a pig did his work in his own skin and a dog in its own. Because I was going to a school here and they required uniforms, that's what I was gonna have to do - suffer through this.

"Yes, Grandad!" I said with a resigned sigh.

He folded up the ironing board, then wrapped the cord around the iron and then tucked them away in his bedroom, then reappeared.

"You goin' eat?" He asked but it wasn't really a question because there was food on the table already.

"I don't really eat breakfast before school."

"Don't be no fool," Grandad said. He moved around the kitchen, making clanking noises in the sink. "You gah tu eat before you go inna dis world, if you ain't got no fuel in you tank, is way you gon' go?" He asked but it wasn't really a question. At least I didn't think that he was expecting an answer from me.

I sat down at the table because it looked like he wasn't gonna take me to school if I didn't. Not that I really wanted to go to school, but I didn't want to stay here either. There were fried plantains in one plate without the paper towel that Ma usually puts them on. There was oil all over this plate. A full avocado with its skin on sat alone on a large plate. It wasn't even cut up but there was a knife next to it. I guessed I'd have to cut it myself if I wanted it! A long loaf of bread waited inside of a see-through plastic bag. A piece of it was already gone because its rough edges at the end peaked through the bag instead of the knotted end of the bread that was usually there. A long sausage laid next to that. Grandad went all out. I didn't know who he thought was going to eat all of this food but it sure wasn't me. There was also a bowl of oatmeal and a cup of tea on the table. The table was entirely too small for all this food but Grandad somehow made it all fit although it made the table look crowded.

"Grandad?" I said, "I don't really eat none of this stuff."

"Bwoy, you not leaving here without some-ting in you belly." He was stern but not scary anymore. "You naw go drop dung pon de people dem school fa dem tu go call me."

"Grandad," I plead. "I promise I do this all the time."

"Eat sum-ting," he demanded. "You got porridge!" He listed the foods on the table.

"Oatmeal?" I asked.

"And pear..."

"Avocado?"

"Plant-tins," He said in his deep accent.

"Plantains?" I laughed but Grandad's face was unmoved. He didn't get the joke. Most of these things that he told me about had different names in Orlando. I didn't know why they were different here when it was the same language. I chased a slice of the plantain down with some tea. It went down like lava, probably scalding the walls of my throat. I took a spoonful of the oatmeal. Yuck. I was definitely not finishing that.

"Thanks, Grandad!" I said and moved away from the table like I ate a feast.

"Tek dis!" He gave me a backpack. It felt like it weighed a ton, but I put it on my shoulder like it wasn't really heavy then I followed him outside. He went to the side of the bus that should've been the passenger side in Orlando and got in to drive. I jumped in on the opposite side. He drove through the gate after clicking on a remote to open the gate then clicked on it when we got through. This ticked me off a little bit because I hadn't even realized he had this thing and if he did, why hadn't he use it?

"Grandad?"

"Hm?" He answered without really opening his mouth.

I wanted to ask him why he had me getting out the bus to open the gate when he knew he had a gate opener but instead I asked, "Do you happen to have an iPhone charger?"

"A wah?"

"A charger for my phone."

"Wah you need a charger fa?"

"Ok," I say. "So? no charger? What about the WiFi password?"

"De Who?" There was a genuine questioning look on his face. He really didn't know what I was talking about. No charger. No WiFi. I closed my eyes for the rest of the ride to the new school. I couldn't even think about Ma right now and why she would even do this to me.

At the school, there were all sorts of kids that looked like me in their khaki long pants, brown collared shirts, their brown belts, and their completely brown shoes. They all moved in unison, like a herd of brown and green going to get slaughtered. They all seemed to know exactly where they were going and why. Me? I definitely didn't belong here, uniform or not. I didn't make a move out of the bus. New school meant that I had to make new friends and I wasn't good at nothing new. Not new schools. Not new friends. I just wanted to keep my head down til my suspension was up. Play this game that Ma dragged Grandad into.

"You naw move?" Grandad asked.

I sighed and jumped out the bus. Grandad jumped out too. I followed him back to the school's office, walked in with the rest of the kids and Grandad, the only adult. It was different this time though. This time I wore a uniform like everybody else. This time I had a backpack like everybody else. This time, I fit in. All the kids were wearing what I was wearing; they were all headed in the same direction, towards what looked like a courtyard, the place with the stage. This was better for me, not standing out. Kept less eyes off me. Blend in. Stay low, I reminded myself.

We headed to the office, right next to the courtyard. It was a sea of brown and green uniforms and I wondered if this were all the kids that went to this school. If so, and my school and this school had a war, the kids in St. Kitts would be outnumbered for sure. The sea of brown and green uniforms faced a large concrete stage. Two kids stood on the stage directing the brown and green sea, one skinny tall dude wore long khakis like what I wore and a girl in a green pleated skirt with her brown shirt. They all recited what sounded like the *Our Father Prayer*, but I wasn't sure because their thick accents said it so perfectly like soldiers marching in unison. Seemed robotic to me but, then again, this wasn't my school.

In the office, Grandad whispered something to the same man that I wouldn't take his schedule from. All I heard Grandad say is *it gon change by mawning*. Who knew what they were talking about this time? The man and Grandad drew closer to me and I realized he was wearing a different suit from the first time I saw him but he was still not hot. Small beads of sweat rolled down my face and I wasn't even wearing half of the clothes this clown wore.

"I am Headmaster Turnbull!" He extended his hand. His accent was as deep as Grandad's but he sounded more like Ma when she spoke to people who may not be able to understand her deep accent. His words were slow and careful. I extended my hand to shake his. His hand was rough and hard like the paper bags we got from the grocery store.

"Kadeem Johnson," I said.

"Mr. Kadeem Johnson!" He repeated my name like I didn't hear what I just said. "We're glad to have you in our school."

"I won't be here long," I said with confidence.

"Whatever time you spend here," Headmaster Turnbull waved his hand to indicate the school, "we at Crayon High School want it to be successful."

"Sure," I said with as much energy as a turtle racing a rabbit.

"Ok, it look like you gon' be fine," Grandad said reaching into his pocket. He pulled out some silver coins and handed them to me. "Dis fu you lunch." Then he left.

"Your grandfather is precisely right," Headmaster Turnbull said. "We understand that you're joining us from the States so this may be a little different for you."

I nodded. *Different* was not quite the word I'd use but, whatever.

"First thing," Headmaster Turnbull continued, "I've talked to your grandfather about your hair."

"My hair?" I questioned.

"Yes, it is in violation of our dress code," He looked at my hair disapprovingly. "Your grandfather assures me that your hair will be in dress code by tomorrow."

"Yo!" I shouted, now agitated and defensive. No one's cutting my hair, I wanted to shout. But, then I calmed down because I remembered that this was just Ma playing her game. My suspension was gonna be over soon. I was gonna be back in Orlando soon. I was gonna have WiFi soon. This was all gonna be over soon.

CHAPTER 6

Headmaster Turnbull walked out the office and I followed him. The sea of green and brown uniforms was gone. Everyone was in their classes. I held the paper that he gave me with as little care as possible and it escaped my hand. Headmaster Turnbull grabbed it from the ground and handed it back to me.

"You will have to hold on to this until you are accustomed to your classes." Headmaster Turnbull said.

I took it, folded it as small as I could, and put in one of the side pockets of Grandad's backpack that he gave me. I followed him up one short flight of steps to the second floor of one of the long buildings. Another similarly built building stood next to this one and then a long one-story building, created an open square that surrounded the concrete stage. Seemed to be an easy escape but I didn't need to escape cause I wasn't gonna be there long.

He was quiet so I was quiet too. I didn't even think that I'd be interested in talking to this sweat-less man in this suit that made me sweat. We passed by window after window, each opened wide. Students in desks faced the teacher. No one was saying anything, just the teacher at the front of the room talked. The windows were wide enough that a couple of people could squeeze through at the same time, if they really wanted to. I found myself wondering what they did for lock down drills in this school. Where would they hide with all the open windows? But, then, I remembered that I wasn't gonna be there long.

"You have been placed in the fifth form!" Headmaster Turnbull said.

"Huh?" I asked. "What's that?"

"This is our equivalent of your eleventh grade." He continued, "Your grandfather indicated that you have just started the eleventh grade, therefore, we are going to place you in this form until your transcripts arrive."

They were really going all out to make me think that this was actually happening, that I was really going to be staying.

"I won't be here long," I said with confidence.

"Nevertheless, you'll still need to know where you are going to be while you are not here long."

"I guess," I shrugged.

"Guessing a thing is not knowing a thing," Headmaster Turnbull said, "It would behoove you to stop guessing."

"Be-who?" I asked but he didn't answer.

He stopped at one of the opened doors. We would never have our classroom doors opened in Orlando, no way! All the classroom doors were shut in Orlando. Some were even locked. This one was wide open like they didn't have no active shooters on this island. He stepped in so I stepped in too. The teacher stopped talking and every pair of eyes in that room turned on me and Headmaster Turnbull but mostly me cause something told me they'd seen Headmaster Turnbull before and his hot suits. The teacher was a tall, skinny, dark skinned man. He looked like he may have been my age, but he couldn't be, cause he was the teacher. He wasn't wearing a suit like Headmaster Turnbull, just a long-sleeved shirt, tie and long pants. Most importantly, he didn't look as hot as I felt. I knew by now that my arm pits must have been showing rings of sweat. They felt damp.

"Pardon me, Mr. Benjamin," Headmaster Turnbull interrupted. "We have a new student today!" This man really sounded excited that I was here. I had been the new kid at a few schools before but never had an introduction like this. In fact, I don't think I'd ever been walked to class before. It was more likely that I got walked to the office rather than class. This was new, but I still wasn't going to get used to it - this fake niceness. I just kept telling myself that I wasn't going to be there long. As soon as my suspension was up, Ma was gonna come get me and before they messed with my hair too. "He's transferred from the States!" Headmaster Turnbull continued.

I said nothing. Didn't nod my head or nothing cause I was sure this man wasn't supposed to be giving out all my information like this and especially not in front of the entire class.

"This is Mr. Kadeem Johnson." He said it like my name was important or something.

"Welcome, Mr. Kadeem Johnson!" Mr. Benjamin greeted, his voice loud and deep like he didn't even need a microphone. The teachers in Orlando had microphones hung around their necks. "Class?" He asked.

"WELCOME, MR. KADEEM JOHNSON!" The whole class shouted in unison. It was weird to hear my name called like we were in some sort of a movie and these robot kids were all conditioned to do whatever was told to them. God, I knew I had to get out of this place cause this was not a good sign. Ma made me watch this old movie once cause she was in love with one of the characters. The school's faculty was all aliens or something like that and they took over the school. These kids reminded me of that, except, it was the teachers who were aliens in this movie and not the students. This whole thing was like an alien movie to me.

"We have a seat right in front for you, Mr. Johnson!" Mr. Benjamin said. Headmaster Turnbull looked at me and nodded his head to the seat then walked out. I instead walked to the empty seat in the back of the room. I'd already spotted it as soon as I walked in. The plan: go in, lay low til the end of my suspension, get back home to Orlando where I belonged. Before I could put the heavy backpack Grandad gave me down on the ground to make myself comfortable for whatever length of time this was going to be, I heard, "No, this seat," Mr. Benjamin said, "the one in front!"

"I'm nearsighted!" I said. I've used this excuse for as many times as I could remember to be able to sit in the back row of every classroom.

"Perfect!" Mr. Benjamin said and clapped his hands together. "Then the front seat will help you to see even better!"

"Huh?" I asked. "I can't see if I sit up close!" I said. I mean who was he? I just wanted to sit, blend in, or even better, disappear. "Teach your class and leave me alone," I thought, but didn't say. But, he had everyone staring at us and what was happening. I wanted to roll my eyes then and there, but I knew that wasn't going to help.

"Mr. Johnson."

"Kadeem!" I said, agitated. "Just call me Kadeem!"

"Mr. Johnson!" He repeated like I didn't just ask him to call me Kadeem. One thing in Orlando, it didn't matter what your name was, teachers always asked what you wanted to be called. This dude didn't budge. "Nearsighted means that you are incapable of seeing objects from afar. Sitting in this seat," He pointed to the front seat, "will be the best choice for you." I dragged myself to the front seat making sure that my feet noisily dragged against each part of the floor I stepped on. Once there, I slouched. I already couldn't wait to leave this guy's class.

Mr Benjamin turned to write on the board but talked at the same time. "You've joined us just in time, Mr. Johnson." Dude, leave me alone. He did not help with this plan of blending in at all. "Just as you walked in, we were discussing *orders of operations*." He spun back around, "tell us your order of operations, Mr. Johnson!"

Dude, really? I was sure that this could be considered bullying. Here I was, my first day and he did not make me feel welcomed at all. I felt like he was putting me on the spot.

He and the entire class waited so I said, "Huh?"

"Numbers are numbers wherever we are in the world. Some may say the same number in a different language, but it is the same number nonetheless." His gaze moved from me to the entire class. "We also use the same order of operations all over the world to arrive at the correct answer." He gazed at me again. "I'm simply asking for you to share the order of operations with the class." He turned to the board and printed $6^2 \times (8 - 6)$. "How would you solve this in America? What would be your order of operations?"

He waited for an answer, so I said, "I don't know."

"You do know," he encouraged.

"I don't!" I shot back.

"All right," he said. "If you don't know the order of operations, then tell us the answer." He handed me a white piece of chalk. As soon as I moved out of my seat, Mr. Benjamin plopped down in it as though he was now the student and I was the teacher.

I stood and stared for a moment at the problem written on the board, half thinking about how to solve it and half thinking about how I ended up here. I should have left that last fight alone. Walked away. Stayed out of Dean Monti's office. I could've been murdering zombies in Call of Duty right now. Instead, I stood in an alien classroom. Eventually I scribbled *72* on the board and walked away.

"Good job, Mr. Johnson!" Mr. Benjamin said and I didn't know why it irked me that he called me *Mr. Johnson* but it did. It was almost if he was making fun of my name or something. "But you're not done."

"That's the answer!" I said confidently cause I thought I was at least good at math, Math and defending myself.

"Yes," he confirmed, "but how did you arrive at this precise number?"

"I don't know!"

"You don't know, you don't know, but your answer shows us that you in fact know, Mr. Johnson!"

"Ok, I just know that I gotta take care of the stuff in the parentheses first, then exponents and then the multiplication."

"It is not exactly how I would explain it," he said and moved from my seat. I returned his chalk and quickly sat down. "However, Mr. Johnson's answer is correct. In the United States, Mr. Johnson," his gaze fixed on me again, "you may know the order of operations as PEMDAS, parentheses, exponents, multiplication, division, addition, subtraction. However, here, we call it BODMAS." He wrote this in large letters on the board next to my solved problem. Then he said, "Brackets, orders, division, multiplication, addition, subtraction. Everyone," he stopped and looked at each one of us, rather dramatically, "this is our order of operations. Never forget it!" At that moment, a bell rang and Mr. Benjamin took his briefcase and walked out the classroom leaving us there. Everyone in the class began to talk, everyone but me. I didn't want to admit it, but that felt good, knowing something, being right.

I put the backpack Grandad gave me on my one shoulder so I could head to the next class, wherever that was. At the door, I heard, "Is way you goin?" Her voice was soft and concerning.

"Next class," I looked back and answered cause, you know, it was a female's voice. Plus, I was the only one leaving so she must've been talking to me. No-one else picked up their bag. No one else headed for the door. In Orlando, when the bell rang, nothing kept us from running out in to the hallways. We even packed up before the bell rang cause we knew the schedule. I had also decided that *this*, whatever Ma was doing, I was gonna use it to change so that when Ma came back after my suspension stint, she'd find a new person, new Kadeem. I was gonna do a 180 and Ma was gonna be proud.

"De next class is in here," she said. She was shorter than me so that meant she was really short. Her brown shoes looked just like the ones I was wearing, no difference at all. Our only difference was that she was wearing a green skirt and I was wearing long khaki pants. Her hair was braided like mine but much longer, maybe thicker and not shaved at the sides like mine. Her skin was a darker shade of brown than mine but that may be because she'd lived under this sun longer. I just got here. She wasn't wearing those fake eyelashes that made girls look like they got feathers on their eyes either. The skin on her face and neck were the same smooth brown which meant she must not have been wearing fake-up. No big earrings. No lace front wigs. Just pretty with no help.

"Oh," I said, making a conscious effort not to stare, but I'd looked at her long enough to see just a small hint of green in her eyes that sparkled. I took out my schedule from the side pocket and unfolded it. She was right, no room numbers on the page, just the names of the classes. Headmaster Turnbull didn't even explain that to me. As much as he had to say about my hair, he sure didn't say anything about me staying in the same classroom.

"Yeah, most of our classes is in here" She plucked my schedule from my hand. "Lemme see your schedule." I didn't get a chance to protest, not that I would've. "Yeah, it look like you gon' be in here wid de rest of us til we go to French and Band. Band is up in de band room, de building close to de office. Me no know how day put de noisiest room next to wa 'pose to be de quietest room." As she said that, I was thankful that Ma talked the way this girl did with me, because I knew exactly what she was saying.

"May I have my schedule back?"

"Yeah, yeah," She said. "It look like you going be lost though so you better learn quick."

"I won't be here long!" I said with confidence, hiding my own uncertainty.

"Not wid you hair so for sure." She looked at my hair with surprise, tiptoed and playfully pulled one of my plaits. Her fingers were long and slim with short fingernails. I noticed this because most of the girls I knew wore long, colorful nail extensions, some with diamonds in their designs, not real diamonds, of course. At least I didn't think so. "Me aint even know how day let you in here wid you hair like dat. You people must have some pull."

"Like I said, I won't be here long. No use in me cutting my hair or making any drastic changes," I said. "The most I'll be here is for a week. Then I'm gone."

"Well, while you here. I is Tess, dat's Amanda, and dat's And-tony." She pointed to the two other students in the first row. Everyone else stood but talked, slightly similar to the sound of the market Grandad took me to on Saturday, except there wasn't no chopping sounds. Here, I guessed, teachers moved from class to class instead of the students. Where did teachers keep their microwaves, mini refrigerators, snacks? This was weird for sure. Maybe, the teachers were, in fact, like the teachers in *The Faculty* movie, aliens, while the students were their victims. Either way, I was glad for Tess's help, so I sat and waited for the next teacher to arrive to class.

CHAPTER 7

The class hushed and kids who weren't sitting before rustled to their seats, much like we did when rushing to class. In Orlando, I was late if I wasn't in my seat by the time the bell rang, another stupid rule. I wondered if it was the same here and maybe this was the reason they were scrambling for their seats before the teacher returned. I didn't miss getting pushed in the hallways or pushing people between classes. I didn't miss other kids stepping on my crisp white Air-Force-Ones because they weren't looking where they were going. I didn't miss having to use class change time to use the restroom although every other kid was doing the same thing at the same time. That was one of the stupidest rules they have at school. Did they even think about that when they made rules? Have all the kids go to the bathroom at the same time then write them up when they were late. Dumb! Either way, I didn't miss that. But still I wasn't gonna get used to this cause I didn't belong here. I was there til my suspension was over, or maybe sooner depending on how Ma was feeling.

I looked up and I saw the reason everyone rushed to their seats. It was their new teacher. She walked in the door and looked directly at me. There was absolutely no expression on her face - completely blank. No smile. No frown. Just blank. Good, I thought now she won't put me on the spot like that last guy did cause I didn't know what else I had in me today. She wore a red dress that fell to her knees and buttoned up all the way to her neck like a turtle neck. I noticed this because I was still hot in my short-sleeved shirt and long khaki pants, and I wondered if she wasn't hot in that thing that looked like it was choking her to death. Shouldn't they be hot with what they wore? Her dress revealed none of her body like it did with my Spanish teacher from last year. I didn't even remember learning nothing but *no bueno* in her class. Looking down her cleavage made me forget everything I was supposed to learn. This woman here could lean over my desk and I'd remember everything. Plus, she was older. Probably old like Grandad. Her skin was like a wrinkle factory. Wrinkles screamed out loud from her face probably because her skin was pale, like Bella from <u>Twilight</u> - not the book, the movie. She had a briefcase with her or what looked like a briefcase, except it was soft because it seemed to stretch out further than it was supposed to be. She wrote something on the board. It was in cursive, and I didn't really know how to read cursive because ain't nobody taught me how. It was like another language anyway. So confusing how the letters joined together to create one word, and I don't really be knowing what they saying.

"The English language is an arsenal of weapons. If you are going to brandish them without checking to see whether they are loaded, you must expect to have them explode in your face from time to time." She spoke loudly with a deep and gruff voice. If I wasn't looking right at her when she was talking, I'd think that a man had just spoken. She then grabbed a stack of papers from her soft looking briefcase and slammed it on the desk. It made a loud bang and her briefcase bag was no longer bulging. The sound scared me a little, like a car back firing. Not enough to run, but enough for me to be fully attentive cause I wasn't sure what she was gonna do next and I didn't like that. Plus, I was right in the front row, easy target. She already looked like she would throw something if she didn't like what she heard. She looked mean and unhappy. It was so silent in the classroom that I could hear myself swallow. She turned back around and faced the board again. She continued the cursive.

"What's that?" I leaned over and whispered to Tess.

She didn't respond. She didn't even look at me so I asked again. "What's that, Tess?"

"Shh..." she pressed her index finger on her lips.

I wanted to raise my hand so badly to ask what was going on. It was so bizarre that the entire class was quiet and this woman's back was turned. In Orlando, someone would've already wadded up a piece of paper and thrown it at her. In fact, I didn't even remember a teacher ever turning their back to us because of that. But, this woman, she was fearless.

"Tess?" I whispered again.

"Bwoy, hush you-"

"Ms. Turnbull!" It was the gruff voice - the man's voice that came out of this fearless woman. "Is there something that you need to say to the rest of the class?"

"No," Tess barely breathed.

"No?"

"No, Miss Netty. I aint saying no-ting." All eyes were on the two of them now much like it was with me and the last teacher except Tess wasn't writing on the board.

"What you said is a double negative, which, in actuality, means that you were in fact saying something," Miss Netty said. "So, explain to the class what is this *something* that you were in fact saying."

Tess's face tightened like she was trying to keep herself from crying. She didn't look like she was enjoying this at all. No way did she deserve how this woman talked to her. Tess' lips quivered slightly like she was trying hard not to break down in front of everybody. I knew this feeling. It was a mental place to hide from people to keep from crying, keep from letting people see weakness. She hadn't looked at the teacher in the face one time. In fact, Tess' eyes hadn't left her desk since the words started raining down on her. That was one of the things that Ma always stressed to me: look the person in the eye. If not, it showed that you had something to hide. Show no fear of them. Tess was definitely afraid.

"She didn't say nothing," I said. I didn't remember giving these words permission to leave my mouth but there they were, standing boldly, as if soldiers at attention. "I was the one talking."

"You?" Her eyelids tightened, almost closing, showing just enough of the whites to let me know her eyes were still open.

"Yes," I didn't like how Tess looked and I wanted her to stop looking scared. "You came in here all mad and sh-" I stopped myself. *Think. Then Speak*. I heard Ma's words loud and clear in my head. "You came in here upset and it's my first day, and I wanted to know what was going on. She-" I point at Tess, "been so helpful already that I thought I could ask her."

"Tess?" Ms. Netty looked at Tess disgustingly. "I assure you that *she* does not know what is in fact going on."

"My bad," I said and put my hand to my chest to let her know it was really my fault.

"Your bad indeed, Mr. Johnson," she said. Here was another person that knew my name, another adult. "Fortunately for you, the entire class is going to have to rewrite their essays and resubmit." When she said that, the entire class, except for Tess, groaned in unison. "You are allowed to submit yours for the first time."

I didn't say nothing cause I wasn't gonna be there long enough to even start writing no paper. She got me messed up.

"Make it a good one, Mr. Johnson," She said then began to hand out papers to the students. She threw Tess' on her desk, and Tess picked it up quickly and placed it in her bag. She didn't hide it fast enough cause I saw that her paper bled with red ink.

This class crawled by so slowly that it took all that I had to make sure that I didn't fall asleep. Ms. Netty's voice could put someone whose veins, even filled with Starbucks, to death. My neck almost broke a few times because I dosed off but Tess, thankfully, tapped my shoulder lightly to wake me. I didn't think I wanted Ms. Netty shouting at me to wake me. By the time the class ended, which seemed like an eternity, I knew that every kid didn't know how to write an essay and I knew what I was supposed to write about. What Ms. Netty didn't know though was that I wasn't gonna write nothing cause I wasn't gonna be there long. The bell rang and I was glad to see this wrinkled faced woman fly out the classroom on the broom she came in on. I looked for the schedule to see what was next but couldn't find it.

"You looking for dis?" Tess asked. Students started walking around us and headed out the classroom quietly like they had just come home from work, dragging, much like Ma when she had a rough day at the hospital. I was glad that I wasn't gonna be there long cause already I felt myself starting something with this wrinkled faced teacher. Tess held my schedule still. I hadn't even realized that she hadn't given it back to me yet.

"Where's everybody going?" I asked. "I thought you said that all the teachers come to us."

She nodded her head, "day do."

"But everybody leaving," there were just two kids outside the classroom door. Everyone else scattered.

"It's lunch time," her voice sounded so different from when I first met her, like the cheerleader left her body and a lifeless Goth person took over.

"Oh, my favorite period!" I joked.

She said nothing.

"Thanks for your help earlier," I said. "I would've been walking around this campus like a weirdo."

"Yeah."

"Can you show me where the cafeteria is?" I didn't remember seeing it and that Mr. Turnbull sure didn't talk about it or show me where it was.

"Yeah, definitely," she said. "You can come lunch wid us."

"Thanks!" I said and followed her out where Amanda and Anthony waited.

Down the stairs and through the gate, not even the end of the school day, yet every student plowed through the gate like school had indeed ended. No security stopped us. In fact, there wasn't even security at the gate.

"Where are we going?" I asked.

"To lunch." Tess said.

"Where's the cafeteria?"

"We don't have no cafeteria." Anthony looked back and said. This was the first he spoke to me directly.

"Well, where do you guys eat?" I asked. They'd turned right when we got out the gate of the school. "Are we gonna even have enough time to eat and come back in time?"

"We good!" Anthony said. Amanda smiled at me. He said we were *good* but what did that mean exactly? First off, we were off campus, definitely something I wasn't used to. Off campus in Orlando meant that we were cutting school. Getting caught meant suspension. My stomach felt queasy like when I knew I was doing something I wasn't supposed to and could actually get caught. This wasn't *good* at all. We walked in pairs, Anthony with Amanda and me with Tess. Tess and I followed Amanda and Anthony in silence. We walked in the streets with the other kids, passing houses on both sides. Anthony and Amanda stopped at a house that was hot pink with a brown roof. Kids packed in. Were we about to have a lunch party at this house? A pink iron fence, similar to Grandad's, surrounded the house. Anthony reached over and removed the lock. We all walked through the gate and Anthony replaced the lock.

"Yo," I asked. "This your house?"

"No," Anthony shook his head. "Dis where we getting lunch."

"In a house?" I questioned.

"Yeah, dis way we come every day except when we go to Miss Joy," Amanda said. Her voice was soft and quiet, not like Tess'. Tess' voice was bold, at least when she first spoke to me, not when she was talking to Ms. Netty. I wanted to get that image out my mind and I knew that Tess wanted to forget it too because she still didn't bring it up. Me, I'd still be thinking about it and thinking about how I could get her back and probably ended up suspended. But, she didn't say nothing. Amanda and Anthony didn't say nothing bout it either. So, I wasn't gonna say nothing bout it neither. We walked up the long walkway to the opened door. Other kids inside wore our same uniform except some girls were in green jumper like dresses and some boys were in short khakis. Once we stepped inside, the house that looked like a house wasn't really a house. Pool tables, a counter with a large chalkboard on the wall behind the counter, its menu written in chalk, waited. No one was playing pool though; everybody was at the counter ordering. It was different from what I was used to - a line with the only choice a square shaped pizza. This menu had a whole heap of stuff that I actually love to eat.

"Chicken and chips, please," Anthony ordered. "We gon share it cause is a lot," he told Amanda.

I looked at the menu intently because there were so many choices. I still wanted to order what I wanted in enough time to get back to school on time. I didn't get it. Thirty minutes for food that wasn't on campus? No way we were gonna make it back and although I didn't really care cause I wasn't gonna be there long, I still didn't want to get in trouble in a place where I was sent because I was in trouble at home.

"Is wa you gettin'?" Tess' voice broke my concentration.

I wanted to get chicken and chips too which was really chicken and French fries because that's what Ma called them, but instead I ordered something quick and that was already prepared.

"I'll get a beef patty and a ting."

"Wa?" Anthony said, shocked, "Yankee, you know what you ordering, bwoy?

"Yeah," I said.

"What you know about ting, bwoy?" Anthony asked.

"It's what I'm used to," I said confidently. "Ma takes me to a Caribbean restaurant often enough for me to know I like drinking Ting. It's just carbonated grapefruit juice." I didn't really understand why he was surprised that I knew what to order. It was just food.

The cashier told me the price and I remembered that I had the coins that Grandad gave me. I pulled all of them out of my pocket trying to figure out which was which. The money was so weird looking. I remembered that some were dollars and the others were quarters and smaller coins, but I didn't remember which was which. It wasn't like my money where it was green paper for dollars and cents for coins. This confused me especially trying to find the right amount so quickly. I must've looked lost because Tess stepped closer to me, closing the gap that was between us.

"You gonna need dis." Her breathe lightly touched my skin as she spoke. She took some of the coins from my palm, her long fingers, soft and cool against my skin. "And dis," she took more coins from my palm, her lips parted as she counted and closed slowly but made no sound. At that moment I didn't mind that someone else stood so close to me. I didn't mind that someone else touched me. I didn't mind that someone else breathed on me. At that moment, I didn't mind being suspended.

CHAPTER 8

Tess, Anthony, Amanda, and I walked back to school after lunch which seemed like a really long time in which to eat but I did not complain. Even with no bell, Tess, Anthony, Amanda and every kid in uniform seem to know when lunch ended. With that time, I really could've ordered the chicken and chips that I wanted. Next time, I would for sure. I could really get used to this but why bother, because I wasn't gonna be here long. After lunch, the other classes sped by like a car in the *Fast and Furious* movies. I fought to stay awake. Tess helped by frequently tapping me on my shoulder. I learned. Kept my head down. Didn't say much. Volunteered answers when the teacher looked at me... I was gonna make it out of here just fine. My week's suspension was gonna feel quicker than the way spring break week felt, quick, like it never happened. In no time, I'd be back on a plane on the way out with the island shrinking smaller and smaller the higher and higher the plane rose.

The school bell rang at the end of the day and like everybody else, I headed out the doors, down the steps and towards the gate where Grandad parked. Somehow, I just knew that he'd be there, but I didn't expect to see him in what he wore.

"Dass you grand-farda out day?" Tess asked. He stood out like a sore thumb. Not only was he taller than everybody by the gates, but his clothes stood out in the sea of uniforms. He was the only dang parent standing out front like I was in the third grade or something. Grandad wore jeans cut off at the knee and every thread that could be free, hung loose. His t-shirt had seen better days for sure, faded cream from what used to be a yellowy lemon color and filled with holes and tears. These holes weren't the kind of stylish holes that you found in the shirts at Hollister. These holes were different, like the shirt had seen hard work. Ma would never pick me up from school looking a hot mess like that. She wouldn't even come inside the school wearing her scrubs to pick me up! One time in the third grade Ma came to pick me up in her scrubs. She marched right into the school wearing those ugly things draped to the floor which covered her ugly white Sketchers. I was like, "Ma, why you gotta come get me looking like this?" I remember cause it felt like everybody, even the janitor was watching us, focused on what she was wearing. Just from that one question and I guess the look on my face, she never came to pick me up looking like that again. This was another reason I was so surprised that she got on a plane with her ugly scrubs and her too-white Sketchers.

"Yeah!" I said. Was the island so small that everyone knew each other?

"I thought you was gonna walk home wid us but I guess you got a ride." If I'd known her longer, I'd swear she sounded disappointed but I didn't want to read too much into it.

"Yeah!" I said. Earlier in class, Tess had said that I could walk home with her and Amanda and Anthony. I didn't normally like walking but I wanted to see what this was like, so I said sure. The island was small enough where it didn't seem like it was a long enough walk to torment me. Plus, I didn't mind her company. Tess told me that she lived in the village south of Grandad's and

Anthony lived in the same village as Grandad so I wouldn't have to walk far and I wouldn't have to walk alone.

"We gon see you to-mara den!" Again, it sounded like she was saddened by my sudden change of plans, but I still didn't want to think too much of it. They disappeared into the swarm of uniformed kids, and I walked towards Grandad.

"You ready?" Grandad asked as I got closer to him.

"Yeah, Grandad!"

"Yes, Grandad!" he corrected.

"Yes, Grandad!" I repeated. Though I slept a lot in class, or at least tried to, I was too tired to try to be defiant. Plus, I wasn't gonna be there long so I didn't want things between us to be unpleasant. Grandad walked behind Tess and the hoard of other students that streamed away from the school. We walked longer than I thought we should have to, unless Grandad parked his van someplace different than he had before.

"Where's your van, Grandad?" I asked.

"In me yard, way it 'pose to be." He left the van at home, *his home*, which meant that we were, like the rest of the people in front of us, walking home. I noticed the hill in front of us and put the straps of the backpack over both of my shoulders just so that I'd be balanced. I didn't notice that hill coming to school. I didn't notice it coming from the airport. But now, here it stood tall and bold like it was the steepest thing ever. It was. It was the steepest hill I would ever climb. Tess, Amanda, and Anthony were within earshot so I didn't want to complain. I didn't want to seem like I wasn't used to walking home from school. Plus, it was so hot it seemed like the heat of the sun made the hill steeper. My underarms were sweating, dampening my shirt. The street seemed narrower than it had in the van. In fact, it seemed choked with all the school children on both sides heading in our direction. Busses whizzed by us one after the other; no one seemed to be afraid that one may somehow veer into the crowd. With Grandad to my side, some of the tallest looking grass I'd ever seen crowded the roadside. Grandad's silence killed me.

"Grandad, why is there fields and fields of grass wherever we go?" There was. I'd noticed them since we'd gone to the mountain. If not grass, then a house.

"Grass?" Grandad sounded skeptical. "Is wa grass you talking bout bwoy?"

"This thing!" I dragged my hand against it as I walked. "Ouch!" I yelped and Tess looked back at me and grinned.

"Bwoy, be careful!" he commanded. "Dis here is sugar cane." Grandad stopped and broke off a piece from the plant. What he broke off looked like grass but then he quickly peeled off the long green material revealing what could pass as a rod or a walking stick with brownish skin on it.

"Grandad," I whispered, "can you do that?"

"Do wa bwoy?" He then put the rod-like thing in the corner of his mouth and pulled off the skin with his teeth.

"Grandad, you can't just take people's stuff."

"Who is people?"

"You know, the people who own this stuff."

"How you know I ain't people? How you know I ain't own dis stuff?" he asked. The truth... I didn't know. Maybe Grandad was super rich, and he just chose to live in his two-bedroom house, with one bathroom, with no air conditioning for absolutely no reason at all.

"You're right, Grandad," I gave in.

"Dis ting coming up from de grung," Grandad continued. He chewed on the cane. "Who gon tell me dat I cyaan tek it." He sucked his teeth and chewed. He then offered me a piece but, I refused. I didn't want to be a part of whatever he was getting involved in just in case he wasn't really super rich and actually didn't own this cane. I was already in my own trouble and didn't want things to be worse than they already were. Plus, I didn't want to eat a grass covered rod. Grandad would not give up. He kept pushing it towards me. Finally, I bit into it like I saw Grandad do, on the side of my mouth. It was hard. I imagined if I'd bit into it with my front teeth, it could probably yank them out. I didn't want to go back to Orlando toothless like a hockey player! I peeled the skin off just as Grandad did to reveal a cream-colored rod. I bit into it like Grandad did but I couldn't get it to separate like it did for Grandad so I just chewed on its top. It was sweet and juicy.

I stopped chewing long enough to say, "This is good, Grandad, but it's sweet."

"Is wa you expect?" he asked but he wasn't expecting an answer cause the sugar cane was back in my mouth. It was like drinking refreshing sweet water. "Is sugar cane, ain't sour cane you eating."

The juices ran down my forearm, off my elbow and onto my shirt.

Grandad warned, "Do-an let dat drop pon you cloze eh!" But it was too late. It was all over my uniform. "You gon just gah tu wash it when you get home cause is de one uniform you got." I smiled when he said that. I didn't know if he noticed but he pretty much confirmed that I wasn't gonna be there long. One uniform? No way was that gonna last me; I saw their game, Grandad and Ma. Right then the sugarcane started tasting sweeter and sweeter as we walked.

Turned out, we weren't the only ones eating the sugar cane. The other children walking home from school were too. They yanked stems out of the field, breaking it off piece by piece, peeled it, chewed it up, and discarded the remains on the ground. Did they own it too?

"Later, Kadeem," Tess waved. Her green uniform skirt disappeared down a narrow alley. I waved back and smiled. Anthony and Amanda kept on walking ahead of us, a part of a bunch of other kids. The village before us meant we were almost home, Grandad's home anyway. Places started to look familiar. For instance, once we passed the basketball court on the right, that meant that we were closer to Grandad's. After passing the court, Grandad turned through someone's unfenced yard. Anthony and Amanda had already walked ahead of us on the same path. No way I was doing this in Orlando for fear of a dog, the owner, or even the cops, but here it was nothing! Clothes on the line hung out to dry. The path was worn; a few wisps of grass proved that Grandad wasn't the only one taking that path on a regular basis. Turned out, it was a shortcut to Grandad's and I was glad cause even though the sugarcane was good, the sun was still too hot even to be outside, never mind walking home from school. Tess was right. Anthony and Amanda veered off one of the many streets of Grandad's neighborhood. They didn't wave bye like Tess did but that was okay, I guessed.

Why did Grandad's house have to be on the top of the hill in this hot sun? Another hill to climb, but once there, it was good, cause it was like all the breeze from the ocean blew our way. It felt so good that it almost made me forget that I'd just walked a hundred miles to the house in the hot-ass sun. Grandad didn't appear tired, but the sun seemed to have sucked all the energy out of me. He sauntered into the yard and around to the back of the house like it was nothing. Both vehicles sat idle in the yard. That annoyed me cause the only time I got a whiff of some ac was when I was in one of those vehicles. He could've totally picked me up in one but whatever. I followed him around to the back of house. Was something wrong with the front door? The only time I'd seen him use it was when me and Ma arrived that night. Since then, it had been locked and covered with a curtain like it was a secret door or something. His back door, though, was wide open. It looked like it'd been open the whole time he was out. No way, I thought. There was no way we would do that in Orlando! Opened door while gone? We didn't even leave the door unlocked when we were inside much less leave it wide open when we were gone. This was no doubt reckless. Grandad took out a large tub from the tiny house in the back of the yard. I called it a tiny house because I'd never been in there and I'd seen that *Tiny House* show with Ma enough times to form an idea of what it could possibly contain. He filled the tub half full of water and placed it on the ground.

"Tek off you cloze," Grandad commanded.

"What?" I asked. We were in the yard and the fence was not tall enough for me to undress behind. Neighbors lived further up the hill, people who could see right into the yard.

"Tek dem off and put dem in here," he said nonchalantly pointing to the tub. He was serious. I thought about protesting, going into the house, changing into my joggers and t-shirt, and bringing the uniform out, but I thought against it. I didn't want Grandad to get upset with me and give Ma a bad report either so I just peeled off the uniform. I wore boxers so I wasn't completely naked.

"Here," I said and handed him the shirt and pants but I still felt uncomfortable in the yard without clothes.

"Why you a ge dem to me?" Was Grandad asking me why I was giving him the clothes? I wanted to say, *hey, you asked,* but I knew better. Was I on the road to making better decisions? By the time I got back to Orlando, I was gonna be a whole new dude. "Me no wear dem!" Grandad continued.

"I know you didn't wear them, Grandad, but I thought you asked me for them so that you could wash them."

"You tinking wrong again." Grandad left the tub of water on the ground and went back into the tiny house. He emerged with something that looked like a large cutting board and the bluest bar of soap I'd ever seen.

"What's that, Grandad?"

"Dis is how we wash." He submerged part of the wooden board into the water while the rest of it rested on the edge of the tub. "I don't know wat Gwendolyn up dere teaching you if you never wash you own cloze before."

"I do my own wash, Grandad." This was partially true because I'd collected whites and my colors when I had enough, and Ma would wash them, fold them and put them on my bed.

"Good, cause you gonna do you own wash while you here," he stated matter-of-factly.

I leaned over the tub in the same manner as Grandad, but on the opposite side. He dipped the shirt in the water so that it was soaking wet. Then, he rubbed some of the blue soap on it. "Mek sure you no put nuff soap on it aw it gon mess up you cloze." He then put the soap down on the ground, not even on a soap dish. He didn't care that pieces of grass would stick to it like a magnet to metal.

"Watch wa a doin' eh!" he commanded.

I did. He held the shirt in his two hands now and rubbed his hands together with the shirt in between. Then he gave it to me.

"Do it," he commanded.

I did. I dipped the shirt in the water again and rubbed it between my two hands. I kept at it and the shirt started to look clean. The discoloration under the armpits disappeared when I concentrated on rubbing that area; so did the discoloration from the sugar cane juice. I did the same to the pants. I began to feel angry again when I thought about why Ma left me out here basically in the wild to fend for myself. No ac and now no washing machine, not that I knew how to use it anyway, but, damn; I was in a backyard washing clothes in my boxers. If this wasn't enough punishment for something that wasn't my fault, I didn't know what was. Grandad went into the tiny house and got another tub also half filled with water.

"Now you gah tu tek dat," he pointed at the clothes in the other tub that I washed, "and rinse it out, hang it on de wire and pray it dry fa school in de mawning."

I did almost everything he said. I hung the clothes on the line. I did not pray for them to dry cause I didn't care.

CHAPTER 9

"Whaaaat?" I whined. It had to have still been night time and Grandad was trying to wake me. He shook my shoulders violently as though he thought I wouldn't need to use them later or something. "What Grandad?"

"Don't *what* me, bwoy!"

I sighed. It wasn't Saturday so I knew we weren't going to the mountains or to the market. But, man, it was early. I still hadn't heard the rooster crowing, my sign that I needed to get up. If the rooster slept, I should too. My phone was dead by now. With no charger and no wifi, I couldn't even use my regular alarms. Since Grandad didn't have a charger, I just packed it back into the duffle bag so I could bring it back to life when my suspension was over.

"What's up, Grandad?" I wiped the crust from my eyes.

"De sky, a hope, cause if dat ting fall we all in trouble!"

I wore my boxers. I'd stop sleeping in my joggers cause it was just too damn hot. If I could sleep naked, I would, but I didn't wanna scare Grandad. On the other hand, maybe I should. Maybe it would get me home sooner.

"What's going on, Grandad?" I asked wearily. "Why'd you wake me up this early?"

"Bwoy you never hear de ur-ly bud get de wum?"

"Grandad, do you mean *the early bird gets the worm?*" I chuckled.

"Same ting, I say."

It was actually a whole different thing he said but I did not have the energy to argue this morning or whatever time it was. Energy or not, he was going to find some way to assert his old-man-island-type logic anyway, so why even try?

"I don't even know why we're up this early. School doesn't even start til 8 here," I grumbled. "I thought I would at least get a chance to sleep in til Ma comes back."

"You tink-ing wrong again, boy."

I followed Grandad out my room, through the kitchen and out the back door. Where were the clothes on the line? I wondered briefly what he'd done with them, but then realized that I didn't care much. A lone chair from the kitchen sat on the grass with a light shining over it. I hadn't even realized that Grandad had lights in his backyard until now. This one seemed to shine brightly and directly over the chair like a spotlight on a stage. As I stepped onto the grass, my bare feet sank. It must've rained last night. I walked towards the chair, following Grandad, cause this was the only way that I was gonna be able to go back to sleep: do what he wanted so I could get some shut-eye.

"Come sid-dung, right here." He directed me towards the chair.

"For what?" I noticed a bucket right next to the chair, upside down like a makeshift table. On the bucket-table lay long thick-looking silver scissors and electric clippers plugged into a long orange cord that looked like an orange skinned snake squirming from the tiny house.

"Is so you does talk to you mudda?" he asked. I wanted to say I didn't talk to Ma like this cause she didn't wake me up early in the morning for asinine reasons. Probably only the second time I'd ever used the word, *asinine*, I'd been trying to fit in somewhere since the first time I heard it. Once, my English teacher said a kid in class was doing "asinine" things. I couldn't stop laughing cause all I heard was the teacher calling the kid an ass. After googling it, I vowed to use it and Grandad provided that opportunity.

"Grandad," I warned after noticing what was on the bucket. "I'm not cutting my hair."

"Sid-dung!" he demanded but he still didn't shout.

"Grandad," I warned again, "It's not happening." I remembered the conversation that Grandad had with the headmaster, how he said it'd be gone by the next day. The *it* must've been my hair but I wasn't having it. No way!

"Sid-dung!" he grabbed the back of the chair as if steadying it for me.

"Grandad," I was pleading now. "Ma'll be back soon and she won't like this. This is my hair, my style. This is how I go to school."

"You cyan't go a de people dem school wid a burd nest pon you head."

"It's not a bird nest, Grandad!" I protested. "It's what makes me unique. It's what makes me, me."

"Bwoy tap talk tru-pid-ness!"

"It's not stupidness, Grandad."

"So wat you telling me is dat you hair mek you unique?" he asked, but didn't wait for an answer. "You hair mek you who you is?"

"Yes!" I said as soon as he paused.

"So den, if I is to go by you logic, you hair is wat mek you get suspended from de 'Merican school." And just like that, I'd been gotten again by his island logic.

I surrendered and sat in the chair. All I could think about was Ma really taking this too far. This was ridiculous. I was never, ever going to forgive her for this - not even if she took me on a shopping spree to the biggest Nike store in the world. Grandad picked up the scissors from the bucket. I still hoped that this was a joke or a dream but just like when we went to the mountains in the dead of the night it felt like, this, too, was really happening. Everything began in slow motion. It had taken me so long to grow my plaits to their length. I had planned to color the tips auburn when I got back. Now, I couldn't. I still hoped that he would just make the cutting sound, maybe scare me, like in one of the scared straight documentaries. You know, scare them enough so that they never want to see jail again. But no scared-strait tactic, this was happening. Grandad sawed off my long plaits so I could fit into a school that I wasn't going to stay at long.

The sound of the scissors roared thunderously. Each time the shears clacked together, it was like Grandad was using ridiculously large gardening scissors. I could hear each plait screaming on their way from my head to the ground, each one pushed off a cliff, splattered on the ground. I swallowed hard. I wasn't going to cry. No. Not today. But soon, burned at the edges of my eye lids like water out of an unsuspecting small hole in the bottom of a paper cup, each tear slid down the corner of my face, joining the others to make a chain. I stayed silent though. Not a whimper. If this was how Ma saw fit to punish me, so be it. Just when I thought that he was done with this game, he put down the scissors and picked up the clippers. The buzzing sound was loud, like a lawnmower on an early morning. The rest of my hair fell in cascades to the ground joining their comrades in solidarity around the feet of the chair. Ma had done it. She'd really taught me a lesson this time, for sure.

"Dis look better dan when I do me own hair," Grandad boasted. He brushed strands of hair from my shoulders. I rose slowly, like I needed someone to help me up. I didn't put my hand in my hair like I normally did at the barber. I didn't want to look in a mirror. I couldn't imagine what I looked like, who I looked liked. I just didn't feel like I was me any more. I went back into the kitchen. The brown collared shirt and khaki pants lay already ironed, folded neatly over a kitchen chair. I grabbed them on the way to my room. The rooster still hadn't crowed. Grandad's daily obituary radio show wasn't on so it was still early, before a normal time people would get up. Numbly, I took a shower since sleep was out of the question. I had made every decision regarding my hair ever since I could remember. I knew when I wanted it cut and when I didn't. When I asked Ma to braid my hair, she didn't even ask why. She just did. And now, now they were gone. I put on the uniform and went back out into the kitchen. Still, I didn't look at my hair. Still, I didn't feel my hair. Grandad was at the kitchen table by the time I got there, drinking from a big metal cup. A plate sat next to Grandad with waffles and bacon plus a bottle of Aunt Jamina's syrup - a real American breakfast. Was he trying to make me feel better or something? Where was this food before? I swear he be holding out on me, but I wasn't gonna fall for it.

"Bwoy, eat dis food before you go drop dung in de people dem school," Grandad commanded.

"I'm good," I grumbled. I wasn't.

"Wat dat mean?" he asked. "Dat mean, you don eat?"

"Naw Grandad," I shifted the weight to my other leg. "I ain't hungry." This was a complete lie. I was starving. I was always starving for waffles and bacon, no matter what time of day. Plus, this looked real good since I hadn't had it in a while. Plus, I knew that Grandad must've made a special trip to town just to get them. This wasn't what he normally kept in the house for sure, with his plantains, avocados, porridge, and fish. I knew I should appreciate his gesture but I just wasn't in an appreciative mood.

"So-ot you-self den!" Grandad drained the rest of whatever was in his large tin cup then got up from the table and headed out. I followed him holding the backpack he'd given me, wearing the uniform, and now, the haircut he'd given me.

We rode to school in deafening silence. Somehow the ride seemed longer. We passed other students walking towards the school. Didn't they have a school bus here? I stifled my question; I didn't want Grandad thinking that I was interested in anything that they had here. As we got closer and closer to school and the sea of uniforms, I thought about Tess and how she sifted her fingers through my plaits. What would she sift through now? I eyed Grandad from the side and sighed, all the air leaving my body in an exasperated whimper.

"You lucky you got breath in you cuz plenty people don't dis mawning," Grandad said as we pulled up to the gate. Wordlessly, I tumbled from the van so that he wouldn't walk me in as the he did the other day. I tried to walk through the sea of uniforms but had no idea where I was going. "Kadeeeem!" Grandad said my name like Ma did, stretching out the E's. I kept walking.

"Ey!" Tess said. She stood at the edge of the stairs leading to the second floor.

"Hey," I said, hoping that she wouldn't notice my hair. But that'd be like not noticing the Wifi went out while watching Netflix - impossible. I wished I'd looked in the mirror to at least check out what I looked like, see what she saw.

She reached on tiptoe, her hand on my head. My body slouched down so that she could reach more easily. "Dis is different!" She casually ran her fingers over my head. I shrugged. "Kadeeeeeem!" Grandad called again. This must've been normal behavior because no one really looked around or said anything. By now, someone would've said, "Yo, Pops must think you're deaf or something." But, everyone carried on like he wasn't the only adult male with no shirt and tie, shouting out a kid's name. Where was security?

"You no hear you grand-farder a call you?" Tess' eyes widened.

"No," I lied.

"Well, he coming dis way."

I sighed. In Orlando, I didn't think parents were allowed to come on campus without going to the office first. Plus, I knew I ain't seen no other adults picking up or dropping off nobody.

"Kadeem!" Grandad heavily dropped his hand on my shoulder.

"Hey, Grandad," I turned around with the fakest smile I could muster.

"So, you no eat no breakfast, and now you naw eat no lunch?"

"Huh?" I asked. Kids walked around us like we weren't blocking the way, I guessed. The stairs were broad and lots of people climbed at the same time. But, standing was messing up the natural order of things, the natural flow of traffic. "I gotta go, Grandad." With Ma, I would've just acted like I didn't hear her and she would've left whatever in the office. They would've called me down and that would've been the end of it. Grandad didn't operate like Ma. It was like he made his own rules or something.

"Tek dis." He shoved money into my hand like he did the last time with the coins, but this time I held some crumpled paper money along with a few coins. I pushed it in my pocket, then walked away.

"You not gon' say tanks?" Tess asked. I forgot that she stood next to me. No, I hadn't. Who could forget her? She smelled like fresh mint and her lips were shiny and plump with lipgloss. Could she see herself? Her hair pulled back from her face and into a ponytail on the top of her head. I don't ever remember seeing a girl this naturally pretty who didn't have some fake everything. Maybe back in middle school? Her neatly pressed uniform made me feel like maybe I needed to find a dry cleaner or something, just in case Grandad didn't feel like pressing mine.

"For what?" I joked. "Just kidding. Thanks for waiting for me." I was actually relieved that she did wait. I'd already forgotten which classroom to sit in since they all looked alike.

"Me?" She seemed confused. "Bwoy, say tanks to you grandfarder! He just gee you money to buy food wid! You should be grateful."

CHAPTER 10

School was not nearly as enjoyable as the previous day. I mean, everything reminded me I was suspended, forced to a new school in a new and different place. Yeah, Tess still sat next to me, but now she didn't say much. Yeah, she let me join the group for lunch, but she didn't count out my money. She didn't stand next to me, touch my hands or breathe on my skin. Even though she was physically there, she wasn't really with me. I had only known her a short time, but I thought that she was gonna make my suspension palatable. *Palatable,* that was the word I wanted, the word the teacher explained yesterday. Anyway, I hoped she'd make my suspension easier to handle. Today I couldn't forget, yes, I was suspended and had to get home and quickly. I could feel the school's walls closing in on me. Even though there were no hallways with kids shoving, everyone was still in close quarters. Whether we were all leaving the school for lunch or leaving for the day, once we escaped the classroom, we were packed together. Outside the classroom doors rolled a long verandah barred by metal railings, I guessed to keep kids from falling over. Some kids sat on them and waited for the next teacher or the end-of-lunch-bell. Not that I'm afraid of heights, it still didn't seem like a good idea to sit on railings. Though not a long drop from the second floor, it was still a drop.

Silence filled the room as she marched in and plopped her soft briefcase on the desk.

Water

Moon

Sunrise

Mother

She scribbled all four words on the board, one after the other turning to the class she asked, "what do these words have in common?"

Silence.

"Water?" she bellowed.

Silence.

"Moon," she added.

Silence.

"Sunrise?" She stepped closer to my seat but did not look down. Another reason I hated the front row!

Silence.

"Mother," she paused. "Nothing?" She walked to the other side of the classroom, leaving me to breathe again. I imagined a pin dropping to draw every one's attention.

"All right," she continued. "What about plantains?" She then walked up to the board and scribbled *plantains* on the board, beneath the other four words. Now, five words were scribbled on the board. What in the world was this teacher talking about? I wanted to say none of these things had any thing in common. Instead, I stayed silent with the rest of the class.

"We need plantains," Tess finally whispered.

"What's that, Ms. Turnbull?" Ms. Netty asked.

At that moment, Tess was that girl who volunteered for her sister in that Game movie. Tess was our tribute. She was going to sacrifice herself for all of us.

"Is food," Tess gulped. "We need food to live."

"And?" Ms. Netty prodded.

"And we need water…"

"Do not begin a sentence with a conjunction, Ms. Turnbull," Ms. Netty interjected.

"Sorry," Tess apologized. No one else said anything. The pin could still have its concert and we'd all still hear it.

"Do not apologize, Ms. Turnbull," Ms. Netty advised. "Do better."

"We need all these things, to live."

"How so, Ms. Turnbull?" Ms. Netty sat on the edge of her desk, the discussion between her and Tess now. Clearly, none of us would get involved. If Tess needed a lifeline, she wasn't going to find one here.

"Well, if you tink bout it, all of dem is needed," Tess paused, "besides de light de moon give off, it does de tides and tells us what time a day it is."

"We have clocks for that, Ms. Turnbull," Ms. Netty pointed out.

"I know we do, but, we no had clocks long time ago," Tess fired back. "I know you no write *sun* on de board, but de sun and de moon does wuk to-ge-da so dat we could know when is night and when is day. So, we need dem."

"Go on," Ms. Netty encouraged.

"I need me mud-da," Tess paused. "I know not erry-body got a mud-da, but not erry-body could see de sun rise, de moon, or water, but day all still needed."

"Very good, Ms. Turnbull," Ms. Netty rose from the desk. "Many times, we don't need something until we lack it." I so badly wanted this class to be over, but she droned on. This seemed the longest class of the day. Finally, she said, "In *Praise Song for My Mother*," Grace Nichols uses certain metaphors to emphasize the necessity of one's mothers. As you read this poem, think about how her Caribbean heritage may have influenced her words."

Ms. Netty gave a copy of the poem to each of us. Great, Ma had these people working for her too. Ms. Netty had a whole poem bout Ma. I thought about Ma and how she'd left me and how I hadn't really needed her til I really needed her. Like now. To come get me out of here!

"You good?" Tess asked.

"Yeah, why?" I wasn't.

"Cause we ga tu come up wid a meta-fa dat show *need* before de timer go off."

I hadn't heard her. I hadn't even seen when she'd set the little white timer on the desk. Where did it even come from? I quickly underlined a couple of phrases but but got stuck at *you were the fishes' red gill*. Dang fish couldn't even breathe without their gills. Was this woman saying she couldn't breathe without her mother?

I thought about Ma again and why I was here. Why was she punishing me, for something that wasn't even my fault? Then, I thought about all the things that I'd put her through: unnecessary fights. I really could've just walked away cause them dudes ain't never touched me. The time I squirted water all over a kid's clothes, soaking him from head to toe. I'd really expected him not to react but before I knew it, everyone was chanting "fight, fight" in the hallway like they do whether the fight's big or not. The time I hit a kid in the back of his head in PE. He hadn't even done anything to me, but I felt like throwing a basketball at him. Before I knew it, a sea of PE uniforms was around us, shouting "fight, fight" till the teacher yanked me off him. But this last fight was not my fault! Just walking the hallway minding my own business and out of nowhere a guy shoved me into the wall. It wasn't crowded, just the two of us in the hallway and he shoved me, smashing my shoulder into the wall. Yeah, I wasn't supposed to be skipping class. He wasn't supposed to be skipping either, but he started it. This time for sure if they pulled the security cam (that they always say they gonna pull), they would see that. They'd see this last time, my innocence.

After class, as the verandah grew crowded, I decided to give it a try. "Walking home, Tess?" I hadn't really expected an answer, at least one that I wanted to hear. Besides going beast mode in class, she'd been quiet. She'd seemed talkative at first, talking non-stop, touching me without permission. Wait! That doesn't sound right. Touching my hair and my hands without permission. Did she not like this haircut Grandad gave me or it was just because I didn't say thanks to him when he gave me money? Either way, she didn't like something, and I wanted to fix it. I didn't know why but I liked this girl, the way she looked and especially the way she smelled.

"We could," she said, "but it look like you gran-farder here for you again."

I looked up; she was right. Grandad waited outside the gate in a fit that was worse than the one that he wore the day before, proof that his goal was to clown me in front of everyone. I shook my head and sighed. Grandad wore another wide-brimmed straw hat that had lost its straws. He probably bought his hats in a bulk store, wearing a different one each time we met. Brown strings blew in the wind, and he acted like he wasn't blocking the path. In loose, cutoff jeans again, his belt blatantly kept the baggy pants up. His faded blue t-shirt had holes, enough holes to be garbage. No question; if Ma saw it, I'd be using it to wash her car. Either way, this wasn't a fit meant to be seen by others. That wasn't the worst of it: the Jesus sandals barely hid the dry skin on his feet. I wanted to ask him if he'd ever had a pedicure as his toenails were brown and thick like they had never seen clippers. I didn't mind pedicures. I enjoyed how the lady rubbed my feet with the stuff she had in her kit. I always asked Ma for the deluxe and she didn't never say no. The only thing I didn't like was when Ma told me I gotta go every two weeks. She made it sound so feminine, so I tried to miss in between and only went once a month cause I ain't no woman.

"Next time?" I asked.

"Next time," she replied. At least that sounded promising. She didn't say no but she could've. She didn't.

We walked out towards Grandad. She waved and quickened her step to join Amanda and Anthony who were in front of us walking home with the rest of the kids. Grandad and I walked in silence. He yanked out cane from the fields, broke one in half and gave it to me. I took it and bit into it the way I saw Grandad do the day before. The only sounds were kids talking, vehicles whizzing by, and me and Grandad chewing on the sugarcane. We finished the sugarcane and threw the chewed stalks on the ground like it was no big deal, like we weren't littering. In Orlando, we'd either get a ticket for littering or sent to jail for stealing sugarcane. Grandad nudged me into the dirt part that separated the cane fields, leaving everybody else to continue. The path was only large enough for one row of vehicles.

"Where we going?" I asked. "It's dusty."

Silence. The buzz of the kids' voices lessened, and I lost sight of Tess.

"Where we going, Grandad?" I asked again.

"We goin' get some food!"

"Food?" Surrounded by walls of sugar cane, tunnels made taller by walking between them, no way could a grocery store be at the end of this path, nor even a market. Grandad don't never gimme no straight answers. We walked for a good twenty minutes, maybe more, the sun hotter than the beginning of the afternoon. The rings around my armpits formed; the dampness dripped down my armpits. The dust from the path started to change the color of my school shoes from the school brown to been-in-the-desert-brown. I was glad I didn't wear my white AirForce Ones. I would've taken them off for sure coming down this dirt road and walked barefoot to save them.

We reached a point where the path seemingly ended. It widened, much like the path on the mountains, but instead of revealing a garden, there lay the crystal blue ocean and endless white sands. It wasn't as though I'd never seen the beach before. I had. We lived in Florida where a beach lay only a couple hours away in either direction. Cocoa Beach was my favorite because the water was bluer than the water in Daytona. This water here, though, was crystal, clear and sparkled, like cuts of diamonds peaked from the ocean. No way this water connected to the water in Daytona or Cocoa, no matter what the maps said. We stepped on the sand where the sugar cane ended and the coconut trees started.

"Ok, good!" Grandad clapped his hands together.

"Grandad, where we gonna get this food from?" There was no grocery store in sight. No market. Not even a hut or stand.

"Eh-ry-where!" Grandad walked farther and farther away from the coconut trees on the sand and closer and closer to the ocean. I followed, backpack in tow. As we drew near, small boats, much like the one from which Grandad bought the fish idly dotted the water. I wasn't talking about small yachts, nothing fancy about these things. In fact, they didn't even look safe to sit in; yet, they waited like the green bikes did, in the park or the side of the street for someone to swipe their credit card and pedal off. I hoped and prayed that this wasn't what Grandad intended. They were each tied to a grounded stake in the sand. Grandad loosened one with ease.

"Grandad." I looked around to see if anyone was coming.

"Why you does complain so?"

"I don't complain, Grandad."

"Den get in de boat den!" Grandad commanded.

"With my backpack?"

"You crazy?" Grandad asked. "Dat gon weigh us dung."

"So, what do I do with it?"

"Throw it dung on de bay front til we come back."

"Just leave it here?" I was skeptical. I didn't just leave stuff anywhere unless it was in my bedroom or my living room. But to leave stuff out the open where anyone could take it? That seemed a bit crazy, even too crazy for Grandad.

"Bwoy, just leave de ting day! You tink people goin roun' teefing school bag? You barely want de ting you-self!" He was right. Who was going to steal a school bag? It's not like it had a computer, phone or iPad in it. So, I did what Grandad said and left it on the sand. "Tek off you socks and shoes too and jump in dis ting. Les go get dis food." The sand was grainy between my toes but soft and warm, almost like little round balls massaging my feet as I walked. I liked it. I didn't tell Grandad, but I liked its soothing feel. The Bob Marley song *Every Little Thing Was Gonna Be Alright* thrummed through my thoughts.

I climbed into the boat, not wanting to be left a shore. Grandad pushed the boat while running and then jumped in at the same time, like I've seen those bobsledders do except that this was a little boat, not a bobsled. The boat shook slightly when he got in, like it was going to topple over. Grandad was right again; the weight of the backpack would have been too much. We weren't sinking, but I could tell that me and Grandad's weight was all that this little thing could carry. The boat was so small and narrow that while I was on one end and Grandad on the other, our feet touched. He rowed the boat with ease almost to the center, it seemed, of the ocean, leaving the shore far behind; the backpack and shoes no longer visible. Grandad stopped rowing and started unbuckling his pants.

"Grandad, what you doing?"

"Going get dis food." He undressed, leaving only his white underpants on. I didn't even think people wore those anymore. The last time I wore those, I must've been in the third grade or something like that. Anyone who wore those to school, they'd get a wedgie in the locker room.

Water splashed into the boat when Grandad dove into the water. I carefully peeped over hoping that I could both see him and not topple the boat at the same time cause I couldn't swim, at least not good enough without my legs standing on something. He quickly popped up out of the ocean and hung on to the boat with one hand.

"Aaaagh!" I screamed as he threw lobsters in the boat.

Grandad laughed.

Still alive, they clamored on top of each other and tried to escape. I pulled my knees in to my chest and held them tightly together hoping that would keep them from biting me or even touching me.

"You de only one I ever see fraid a he food!" Grandad laughed, then he disappeared into the ocean again. How could he leave me with these creatures to fend for myself? They scrambled as I struggled not to get bitten. This was not the fish tank at Red Lobster's. They were right in front of me, no glass between us. Grandad emerged more quickly than the last time and this time plopped in two crabs, also alive. Once Grandad settled in the boat, he picked up one of the lobsters by its back. It moved its claws like it was really trying to maybe fly out of Grandad's hand or something. He pushed it towards my face close enough where the seawater from the lobster dripped on my khakis. "You can't fraid you food. You fraid chicken?"

"No," I whimpered.

"You fraid pig?"

"No."

"You fraid turkey?"

"No."

"Well, den you no 'pose to fraid lobster," Grandad said matter of factly.

"I'm not," I said, but still kept my knees tightly tucked into my chest away from the biting claws of these dangerous creatures.

"Um hum," Grandad said doubtfully. "You tun!"

"My turn for what?"

"To get you food."

"Huh?" I asked. Before I could say anything else, Grandad shoved me out of the boat and into the ocean.

CHAPTER 11

My arms flailed wildly trying to find something to hold on to, to stand on.

"Grandad!" I screamed.

The boat wasn't close enough to grab. Each time my arms hit the water, it stung like the water had somehow turned into a sword slicing into my skin. "Gran..." I tried calling, but water kept flooding into my mouth making the word hard to come out. I started to sink and I didn't know if it was the weight of my clothes or the fact that I didn't know how to swim. I started to think about all the things that I had never done. Was it true what they said, when you were dying, your life flashes before your eyes? You begin to see things from when you were in the womb, when you were a baby, elementary school? I wasn't seeing nothing like that, but I knew I was dying. I knew that this was it for sure. Grandad had not reached out to grab me. He didn't extend an oar for me to grab on to. My nose began to sting. He was gonna watch me die in this ocean and turn into fish food. I started to regret the fights. I could've just been friends with those dudes and not made enemies. If I had, I wouldn't even be here, sinking, dying. So many regrets. Drinking all the orange juice and leaving none for Ma. Using all the Polynesian sauce and leaving only Chik Fila sauce for Ma even though time and time again she told me she didn't like that sauce. Stressing Ma out. Please, I'm gonna do better, change things around, stay out of trouble, get more Polynesian sauces - enough to share. One more chance was all I needed.

I couldn't even see Grandad anymore, not his bare chest with the short curly white hairs or his white undies. Not the boat, not even its bottom. My lungs started filling up with water, choking me, closing, blocking the air from going in and out like it was supposed to. My nostrils were blocked by water too. Water blocked every hole in my body, forbidding me from breathing. I tried to recall what they taught me at the Y. Nothing came back. I was doomed. Then I remembered. I didn't learn anything at the Y, but I did learn something at the Neighborhood Center. You couldn't go on the field trips to the water parks if you didn't learn this. I spent enough summers to have learned something cause Ma paid for me to go to all the water parks. I started to kick my legs, trying to control the water with my feet. In and out, move the water between my legs. Nothing. I finally closed my mouth so that I could hold in whatever breath I had. I saw that one in the movies, but it didn't help either cause every time I tried to close my mouth, salt water gushed in. I tried closing my eyes so that the salt water wouldn't burn my eyeballs, but they wouldn't close as I sank deeper and deeper into the ocean. This was it for sure. This was the last breath leaving my body. My body was limp, weak. The ocean had taken over. Oh, Ma I love you even though you sent me here to die.

I felt a tugging on my waist. Did something come to finish me off and drag me all the way down to the ocean's floor? Was I dreaming? Was someone saving me? Aquaman. Even better, that red headed woman that was with Aquaman but really wasn't, you know what I mean? Eventually, they'll get together like in Aquaman II or something. But her, I wanted her to save me. Maybe she was. I could faintly see the surface of the water as the thing tugged on me some more, dragging me through the water. My mind blurred in and out of consciousness. I wished that I'd just been honest with Grandad and told him that I couldn't swim. I wished. I thought I was being hauled by Grandad, but why would he? He had thrown me overboard. Then I thought a mermaid or the red-headed chick from Aquaman. Yeah, I was definitely dead. Seeing things before I got to the pearly gates. Didn't even get a chance to ask God for forgiveness so he could let me in without problems. I hoped someone told Ma I loved her. Would they say good things at my funeral; talk about how much of a good son I was? At their funeral, everybody was always a saint no matter what they had done in their past life. My head landed on something hard but it couldn't have because I was dead, complete fish food. My chest heaved like something was pressing on it, minute after minute. As soon as my chest felt light, the pressure started again. The pressure repeated then stopped, over and over. Pressure was on my lips as well. I felt air pushing down on my lungs. Pressure on my chest, then blown air through my mouth. If this was heaven, it wasn't fun so far.

I coughed and water pooled out of my mouth onto my chest. My lungs opened. Air, in and out like it was supposed to. Grandad's palm was on the back of my head lifting my upper body. I coughed some more to make sure that every drop of salt water left my body and that I was really alive.

"Grandad!" I coughed. "You just killed me!"

"Bwoy, hush yo mout'!" Grandad commanded. "You ev'a hear a dead man kaffin'?"

Grandad rowed the boat back to shore like it was nothing. Like his arms didn't hurt from yanking me out the water, like he just didn't murder me. I was silent and shivering, not because it was cold but from fright. Ma had to come get me soon. It'd only been a couple days since she'd left. Point made. I was gonna be good - the best I'd ever been. She had to come back for me, and, soon. I didn't really have friends in the O that I could call friends or even miss but I missed stuff. I missed my Playstation. I missed Waffle House, McDonald's, and Popeye's. I missed AC in my classrooms. I wanted to go home. We walked through the villages like we did the day before and through the yard. Grandad had the lobsters and crabs tied together swung over his shoulders. No one questioned him. One person mentioned how big they were but that was about it. Finally in the yard, Grandad strode straight to his little house with the creatures. I went straight into my bedroom. This was too much. I had to escape. I couldn't take it anymore.

"Grandaaaad!" I called.

No answer.

I left the bedroom, walked through the kitchen and called him again. "Grandaaaad!"

"Eh?" He walked from the tiny house carrying a huge black cast iron pot.

"Grandaad," I said "I need to call Ma!"

No answer. He continued towards the concrete fence at the back of the yard. Fire licked the top of pieces of wood. There was no way we could do this in Orlando; Ma would get in trouble for sure. At least one neighbor would call the fire department. Grandad set the pot on top of the firewood and sat in a chair in front of it.

"Grandad," I said again. "I need to call Ma, please."

"People need food and water, not even a roof over day head. Nobody *need* to call day mud-da."

"Grandad, please!" I pleaded. The truth was I wasn't even sure he had a phone. The tv in the living room hadn't been on since I'd been there. He only used the radio.

Grandad lifted the cover off the boiling pot and placed both lobsters and both crabs in; the pot was that big. I imagined them screaming as their shells hit the steaming water. Then he returned to the kitchen. I followed him. Next to the radio stood a stack of books, papers, and envelopes, like a bunch of mail that he hadn't yet opened. Ma had a table like that too, one where she put all the mail that "didn't need to be opened right away" as she said. Though that table became more and more cluttered over the years, she kept putting more and more stuff on it. She must've gotten that habit from Grandad cause he had the same thing here. He tugged on an object that was still attached to its cord, a white cord under all that mess.

"Stand here and call you mud-da from dis," he commanded. "Me don't want it to move from here cause de last time a lose it."

Grandad handed me an iPhone. A freaking iPhone! Which meant he had a phone charger and most importantly, WiFi. I didn't know what made me angrier, the fact that he just murdered me or the fact that he lied to me this whole time.

"Grandad?" I asked in shock. "I asked you...you know what? Whatever."

I carefully took the phone cause it didn't have a case on it. Reckless, if you asked me. Ma don't never give me my new iPhone til it had a real ugly case on it. That way I could drop it many times without breaking. I looked at the phone like I'd never seen one in my life, checking the back of it to make sure Grandad didn't just gimme a dud. It worked. I touched the screen and it lit up like it was filled with new life. My eyes brightened. Grandad left the kitchen back to his backyard cooking. I dialed Gwendolyn, Ma for short, using FaceTime cause I wanted her to see my face. I wanted her to see my pain. It rang until it didn't and said that *this person is not available for FaceTime.* I dialed again.

"Daddy, I'm at work!" Ma sounded rushed.

"It's me, Ma!"

"Kadeem?" She looked surprised. She was wearing those ugly scrubs and a cap over her hair. Her eyes looked puffy and red like how they looked when she wasn't sleeping. Good, she was worried about me.

"Ma, when you coming for me? My suspension almost up."

"It's going to be a while before I can get back there, Kadeem!"

"What that mean, Ma? What's a while?"

"A while." She looked behind her like she wasn't supposed to be on the phone, like she was hiding or something.

"Ma! Grandad killed me today!" I whined.

"Bwoy, dead man don't talk. How you on dis phone den?"

I rolled my eyes hoping she could see my worry and fear.

"Ma! When you coming for me?" I asked again.

"Not right now, Kadeem!" She looked around again.

"Ma, I can't do it!" I cried "I'm a be good. No more suspensions. I promise."

"Kadeem, I can't talk about that right now." Her voice was stern like when she was gonna be serious with me and not play at all - Mommy mode, she called it.

"Well, when, Ma?" I whined some more. I'd planned on shedding some fake tears to convince her to come soon but these tears were real, flowing with ease. "My suspension up soon and if I don't get back in school, Imma get in more trouble for missing days."

"Not now, Kadeem! The plan is for you to finish out the year there and we'll see from there. Okay?"

"The whole year?" I screamed.

"Yes, the whole year. This will be good for you and your..."

"Ma, please, I get it, I get it now," I declared.

"You get what, Kadeem?"

"I get what you was trying to teach me,"

"Which is what?"

"Not to fight," my voice softened, "stay out of trouble, I get it so I'm ready to come home."

"You're ready?" she mocked.

"On God, Ma," I raised my hand to the sky, "Imma be good."

"Glad to hear, Kadeem," she looked around again like what I was saying wasn't important, like I just didn't promise her, like she didn't even care. "You're staying there! We've already decided."

"I don't even live here!" my voice raised.

"Try that again, Kadeem,"

"I don't even live here," my voice lowered.

"You live there now, Kadeem," she looked around as though I wasn't her only focus.

"Ma, I don't understand. I thought I was just here for my suspension. It's over in a couple of days," I tried again, "I gotta get back in school."

"You're in school now, Kadeem,"

"Yeah, but this ain't even real,"

"Oh, it's real," she stated.

"Maaaaa," I whined.

"Look, Kadeem, this is where we are at," she closed her eyes and breathed deeply, "maybe Daddy will do what I can't."

"Ma," I whispered into the phone. "Your father tried to kill me today. You know I can't swim, right?" I waited for an answer but she didn't say nothing. So, I continued. "He carried me far out into the sea and tried to drown me. A mean, Ma, I was dead for real!"

"Okay, Kadeem. I've got to get back to work."

"Ma? I died a little." I looked right at her. "Ma, for real!"

"Kadeem, I love you and this is the best thing for you right now."

"Ma! Pleeeaase!" I begged her like I begged when the Playstation 4 came out.

"Goodbye, Kadeem!" Ma said and ended the FaceTime call. She didn't even give me a chance to tell her the good plans that I'd made for when I got home. She just cut me off. I wanted to throw that phone into the wall and smash it to a million pieces, but how would that get me home any sooner?

"You ready to eat?" Grandad asked. I hadn't even noticed he'd returned to the kitchen. He carried a large plate that held both lobsters and both crabs. He placed it in the center of the table. I'm not gonna lie. They looked good, better than the ones at Red Lobster. But I wasn't gonna do it. I wasn't just gonna sit there with him like he and Gwendolyn weren't trying to ruin my life. I wasn't gonna sit there like he didn't just try to kill me. No, thank you! I would starve to death first. I was not gonna spend an entire school year here. Not me. No way.

"No," I finally responded. "I'm good."

"Belly gon' buss before food waste in dis house," Grandad said and started eating.

I wasn't in the mood to sit with Grandad, and I definitely wasn't in the mood to eat. I walked into the bedroom and away from Grandad, his iPhone and his Wifi. Bang! It sounded like a lone firecracker. The door hit the frame so hard that the chest of drawers shook. Gwendolyn and Grandad weren't going to win this one. My plan: wake tomorrow to fight another day.

CHAPTER 12

I'd finally fallen asleep after Gwendolyn basically hung the phone up on me. Not basically. She did what she did. She didn't even really let me explain. Maybe she didn't even care about me anymore. Plus, no decent cereal anywhere, no milk in the refrigerator, just Heinekens. Did Grandad even drink water? I tossed and turned all night thinking about how I could get back to Orlando and if I did, where I would stay since it was obvious that Gwendolyn didn't want anything to do with me anymore. *It's what's best for me* she had said. Yeah, right. How could this be best for me? How would she even know what was best for me? A weird sound broke my not-so-deep sleep, like someone drilling into a piece of wood right next to my head. I hadn't heard the rooster crow yet, so if I had to bet, it was probably still very early, not even morning yet.

I willed my eyes to open. Grandad was busy at work using an electric screw driver, unscrewing the hinges of the door of the room.

"Grandad, what you doing?" I yelled over the loud noise.

Zzzzzzzzsss.

"Good morning, Grandad!" I yelled, remembering his fuss about a proper greeting. I was gonna have to deal with this mess for the rest of the school year, bout eight more months. *It was what was best for me* according to Ma. Gwendolyyynnnn! I wanted to scream but couldn't. I would never dare call Ma anything other than Ma, even if she couldn't hear me. I felt like somehow, she'd be able to sense my cry, sense it even if I whispered "Gwendolyn."

"Good mawning, Kadeem," Grandad said pleasantly.

Zzzzzzzzsss.

"What you doing?" I sat up on the bed cause there was no way I was gonna be able to go back to sleep. I almost wished that school here started earlier like in Orlando. The funny thing is that I used to hate how early school started back home. It was like school started at night. When I left, outside would be pitch dark except for car lights. I used to complain about getting up all the time, but now I wished for it, so I could have some place to be other than here with this craziness.

"Tek-ing dis ting dung!"

"Why you taking down the door?" I asked. "Something's wrong with it?"

"De door fine."

"Then why you taking it off?"

The rooster piped his crow right under the window into the room that I was sleeping in. It wasn't that early after all. Time to get up, to get ready for this school that she, Gwendolyn, left me. After Gwendolyn cut me off, I thought a lot about it last night, what I was gonna do. The plan? To be extra good here. Go to school every day. Do their school work. Get in no trouble. What about that stupid essay I had to write? Grandad could tell her how good I was doing and she was gonna shorten my sentence. Cause that's what it felt like. I'd never been to jail but, for sure, this was probably what it felt like. Trapped. Forced to go to a place you didn't choose. No freedom to go where you wanted when you wanted. That's the definition of jail, right? So, this was jail here. Escaping was gonna be difficult.

"You no know how to close a door de right way so a gon' help you out wid it." Grandad interrupted my thoughts. Did this man really think that I was about to stay in this room without a door? Ma would never even try me like this. I don't even think Ma knew how to use a screwdriver. First, he tried to kill me, now this?

"Grandaaad," I whined.

Grandad gave the bolt one final zzzzzzzzsss, lifted the door off the hinges and carried it outside. Sitting on the bed, in a bedroom with no door, even prisoners had doors on their cells. But me? I got none.

I got ready for school with no door. Dressed in the bathroom, knocking my elbow on the door a couple times because the bathroom was so small. That was okay though cause I wasn't gonna give Ma and Grandad the satisfaction of letting them know that this was bothering me. Fully dressed holding the backpack, I marched to the kitchen where Grandad had a breakfast feast set on the kitchen table: plantains, stewed codfish, boiled green banana, oatmeal, hot tea in two different mugs, and, most importantly, a plate filled with bacon. With a handful of the bacon I headed out the door. Grandad stood in the back yard on a stool to pick golden apples from the neighbor's yard. I shook my head. Ma loved these things. Why they called them golden apples, I didn't know. I didn't love them like Ma because never mind the name, they weren't apples. Didn't taste like apples. Didn't look like apples. Not quite yellow, not quite orange, they looked little oval shaped balls. I remembered when Ma made me taste one. She didn't say quite what they were but all I remembered hearing was the word "apples." Why not, right? I bit into it and spat out a grainy meat-like substance. A combined taste of an orange and green apple seized my tongue and refused to let go. Never again.

I bit my tongue and hesitated, "Grandad, you not gonna get in trouble for that?"

"Fuh wa?"

"Grandad, you on a stool," I pointed out, "picking fruit from someone else's yard. This is technically stealing."

"Bwoy, hush," he commanded. "You see me over in de people dem yard?"

"No." Well, he was in his own yard, standing on his own stool. But that tree wasn't exactly in his yard. The branches that extended into Grandad's yard weighed down the tree so much that several drooped into Grandad's yard.

"So how I teefin' from dem?"

"I'm ready for school." I announced ignoring his weird logic, wanting to get this thing over with. If my plan to get back to Orlando was gonna work, I was gonna have to start now. Act like I care about school. Show a solid change so Grandad would call Ma on his iPhone with his wifi and report how good I was being so I could get out his way. Then, Ma would definitely come get me and it'd be deuces to this place. There was no way Grandad wanted me here. With his failed attempt at murdering me, not even getting my type of food, and now, not even allowing me a door for my bedroom? Naw, he didn't want me here. I really needed to go, return home where at least me and Ma could work things out.

"Not today," he continued to drop golden apples into the bucket next to the stool. It was almost filled with the things. Who was gonna eat all of those? "You friend out day a wait fuh you."

"My friend?" I wondered. I put my other arm through the strap of the backpack and straightened it up on my back leaving Grandad to the non-thieving of his golden apples. I guessed he figured I knew the way to their school today.

A neat ponytail on the top of a head greeted me. She leaned up against the fence, her back towards me.

"Hey!" I said a little too excitedly.

She turned around quickly, like I'd startled her.

"Good mawning," she said and smiled like she was actually happy to see me.

"Good morning," I smiled back.

"A figure a would come walk wid you to school, give you grandfarda a break."

"Nice." I fumbled with the lock on the small gate and met her on the other side. I tried to be cool but after the night I had, she was a welcomed surprise. As we walked down the hill through the yard that Grandad and I used, she didn't say anything. Other kids in uniform walked towards the school too but no one I knew, not Anthony, not Amanda. Finally, I couldn't take the silence anymore. "I thought you lived in this village." Though the villages were within walking distance, I knew she had to come out of her way to walk with me.

"Yeah!"

"So?"

"So wa?"

"So, why'd you come all the way up here to get me?"

"Bwoy, it's not *all de way*," she pronounced very clearly; that special feeling I had kinda disappeared. "You live just up de street from me."

"Ok, ok." I said, and the silence returned until we got to the top of the hill outside her village.

"So, why you here? You hiding from somebody?" She laughed nervously.

"What you mean?"

"You in de witness protection program or some-ting?" Her face was serious.

"Naw"

"I does watch a lot of police show. You just come here almost in de middle of de school year. Dat just seem weird. No?"

"I guess it's strange." I kicked a stray rock that was in the street. "Depending on who's looking at it."

"I looking at it and I say is strange. Erry-body know you come from de states. What happen to you why you here?"

"Nothing." I lied.

"Right," she said doubtfully. "Nothing bring you here. Okay."

I thought I liked this girl who'd been so kind to me on the first day for no particular reason, introducing me to her friends, allowing me to eat lunch with them. In any other school, I would've been a loner and stayed a loner. She made my days go by faster, but did she only come to walk me to school because she wanted to get into my business? Though it wasn't any of her business why I was there, I decided to tell her anyway.

"My grandfather tried to murder me yesterday."

She laughed.

"He did!" I said trying to convince her. "He threw me into the ocean and left me for dead." I decided not to tell her that he gave me CPR and saved me because that wasn't important. At least I didn't think so.

"Wa you tellin' me is da sweet ole' man try to kill you?" She laughed harder this time. "Bwoy, doan mek me laugh."

"He did," I said. "Seriously."

"Okay, how he try to kill you and you still here today? Cause you naw mek no sense." She put her hand to her mouth like she was stifling another bout of laughter.

"He took me out in the ocean in a boat and threw me overboard."

"And?" She waited for more.

"And?" Unbelievable. Was this normal in this country? Attempted murder of a minor? "And, what?"

"Yeah, and what else? Me aint hear de murdering part, cause may I point out that you in front a me standing up like live people do." She laughed again. "Dead man doan walk and talk you-no?"

I shook my head in disbelief. No wonder Ma didn't believe me. I guessed my story wasn't believable. We walked some more in silence. As we passed the cane fields, I considered pulling a stalk from the field like Grandad always did, but I didn't. Just my luck, I'd pull the cane out and slice a finger or two off. I didn't want her to laugh again so I just pulled on the straps of my back pack giving it an extra straighten. Vehicles whizzed by.

"My mother decided that this would be the best place for me right now." I broke the silence.

She nodded her head.

"School wasn't going so great up there."

"Up where?"

"Orlando."

"Dat's where Disney Land at, right?"

Disney World, but I didn't correct her. "Yeah!"

"You ever been?"

"Yeah, a couple times."

"That must be nice."

"Yeah."

"So you mudda just decide out of nowhere that dis was de place for you? Dat doan mek no sense."

"Well, not exactly."

She nodded her head and waited.

"I was kinda getting in trouble." It sounded bad once I heard my words. "A lot."

"Witness protection kinda trouble?"

"No," I laughed nervously. "Suspension from school kinda trouble."

"Suspension? Fuh wa?"

"Fights."

"Naw. I doan believe dat." She stopped walking to stare at me. Other kids passed by us on their way to school too but paid no attention to us or our words. "You doan even seem de type."

"I'm not really." And I really believed that when I said it. "I just think Ma overreacted. I came home one day and she was just packing my shit up with no explanation. Next thing I knew, we was on a plane and landed here."

"You aint never been here before?"

"Yeah, but when I was younger." I did come here several times with Ma just to visit Grandad, but Grandad was never so mean.

"So, you gon' finish off school here?"

"That's *their* plan."

"You no sound too happy bout it."

"I'm not, not really."

"Wa you missing up de're that we doan 'ave here?"

I thought about it for a good while. We started walking again because if we didn't, we were gonna be late for school.

"Nothing, really," I finally said, but the truth: I was really missing my Playstation, Chik Fila, my phone, wifi, Netflix, and now, my own door to my own bedroom. To be honest, I missed Ma too.

"Look at it dis way: you get a kind of a do over."

"How?"

"You no know nobody here so you naw go get in a no fight. Erry-body here easy going."

"That's true but none of those fights were my fault."

"Dat don't matter."

"Yeah it does." My agitation raised my voice a bit.

She stopped walking again, so I stopped too. At the rate we were going, we were going to be late for sure. I honestly didn't want to get in trouble because getting in trouble wasn't gonna get me home any sooner. She took hold of my hand, her hand soft against mine.

"Not really, cause you can't fix wa happen yesterday, right?"

"No," I said, but I was concentrating more on not letting my hand sweat. Sometimes it did that and this wasn't the time for my hands to sweat. I didn't want Tess to pull her hand from mine. I didn't want her to stop her touch. I didn't want her to take her hand from mine and then wipe it on her uniform skirt. That'd be disgusting. This was not the moment for that. "Don't sweat. Don't sweat," I kept telling myself.

"You could only wuk pon right now. Even future plans you can't really wuk pon right now. Cause tings could always change. Right?"

"Right," I agreed.

"So, choose to wuk pon right now and mek de best of it."

I thought about what my response should be. She'd probably remove her hand from mine if I didn't agree with her. I wanted her hand in mine. I wanted her touch. I liked it.

"Ok," I submitted, securing my hand in hers.

"Best of all, bet you never see a smile like dis in Orlando." She pointed at her face and smiled widely, awkwardly showing all her teeth and gum.

I laughed too and continued to walked to school. She didn't release my hand until we got to the school gate. By then, my hand was sweating.

CHAPTER 13

School done for the day. Classes with Tess done for the day. Lunch with Tess done for the day. Just when I thought I was gonna be able to continue on with Tess, Grandad put the kibosh on that. Again, he waited outside the gates of the school yard. I knew disappointment must have showed on my face.

"You know, plenty of us don't have day grandfar-der to come walk wid dem?" Tess asked but wasn't really waiting for an answer. "Most of grandparents dem wo-king or like mine." Sadness filled her face. "Dead."

I wanted to point out that I walked home from school every day in Orlando without Grandad, and I was fine but I kept that to myself. This must've been the reason she was so cold to me the other day when Grandad called me and I ignored him. It made sense now. She missed her grandparents.

"You're right," I agreed.

"I know," she admitted. "I don't be wrong often, eh!"

"See you tomorrow, Tess!" I gave her an awkward pound, fist to fist, and met Grandad outside the gates.

Grandad stood in his usual not-so-swag clothes. Look, if he was comfortable with it, I was gonna have to get used to it, especially if I wanted to get outta here. We walked with Tess and the others in front of us. Again, Grandad yanked out cane from the fields, enough for us both, gave me a piece and started chewing his. I ate mine too. Sugar cane was sweet and good, the juice still ran down my wrist to my elbows. Grandad veered off again into the field using the same path he did the day before, the path that led to my murder.

"Grandad!" I cried out.

Only the rustling of the sugar fields responded; Grandad, he was silent.

"People know where I am, Grandad."

"Nobody know way me be but God."

"Ma knows you tried to murder me yesterday and she not having that."

"Bwoy, you no tink if I was trying to kill you, you woulda been dead by now?"

"Maybe," I grumbled.

He walked on but I stopped. Looked both ways. The way we'd come looked as though I'd be able to live. The other, not so much. I inched back, hoping that Grandad wouldn't even notice that I wasn't following close behind him. My goal: get back to the street where there were millions of witnesses. Maybe not millions, but enough eyes to make Grandad rethink his idea of murdering me. Grandad's image grew smaller. I was gonna get away, escape, live to see another day.

"Kadeeeem," Grandad called, his voice loud and booming, "bwoy, get down ya befo' you lose you way."

The wind moved through the cane answered Grandad. I had no real plan. Once I'd gotten out to the streets, then what?

"Kadeeeem," Grandad called again. "Bwoy me ain't gon let you keep me from eating you know? Is way you gone?"

No answer from me. My no-plan plan still sounded better than losing my life in this ocean. Surely, they'd give me a ticket if I could make it back to the airport.

"Ok, lay dis cane eat you den." Grandad shouted.

Wait. What now? *Let the cane eat me?* That didn't sound good either. My choices were limited: possibly make it out to the airport, drown in the ocean, or get eaten by the sugar cane. Why'd Ma abandon me here? For real?

Grandad didn't look for me long cause I had to jog quite a ways to catch up with him. He continued to walk so I followed, hesitantly. We ended up in the same place as the day before, on the soft, warm sands with the crystal blue sea in front of us. Grandad took off his t-shirt but left on his cut-off jeans. My hands began to sweat again. Normally, in this heat, I wouldn't hesitate to jump in the water. Florida was hot so whenever Ma took me to the beach, it was a pleasure. The beach was a drive, too. The closet one musta been like two hours or something, Cocoa, or maybe Daytona. Here, we just walked to the beach after school which I guessed was nice or whatever.

"Tek off you shoes and clothes."

"Grandad, I can't swim," I complained. "I'm not gonna do this again where you push me in the water to die."

"Strupes." He sucked his teeth. The last time I sucked my teeth in front of Ma, she hit me so hard upside my head that I never did it again. "You see a boat?"

Actually, I saw plenty. They lined the beach like they did the last time Grandad jumped into one and dragged me to a watery grave.

"I'm not doing it."

"Wa?"

"I'm not doin it." I planted my feet into the sand, school shoes and all, like I thought it was gonna hold me down and protect me from Grandad.

"Kadeem!" His tone was serious. "Sometimes you gah tu 'tand for some-ting, dis time ain't one a dem. Aint no-ting here fe you to stand up for. You gah tu learn to swim or force gon mek water go up hill."

"What does that even mean, Grandad!"

"It mean learn to swim now or drown later. Up to you," Grandad said, "now tek off you cloze so we could be done befo' night fall."

He wasn't even giving me a choice but I guess if I was gonna stay on the island for longer than imagined, I needed to learn how to swim. I still wasn't sure he was the best teacher, especially since he tried to murder me. Opening my shirt, I took each button out of the hole as though I'd never done it before.

"Today, eh," Grandad hurried me.

With my shirt still on but now unbuttoned, I slowly unhooked my belt from my pants and pulled it from its loops.

"Is wa you doin'?" Grandad asked, "you no know how to tek off you cloze?"

Of course, I knew how to take off my clothes. This was something I didn't enjoy doing, being any kind of naked in front of people I didn't know. Especially in the locker rooms, people stared for no reason. They watched you like they didn't have what you had. While Grandad and I weren't in the locker room, this still felt awkward, like wearing the left shoe on my right foot - uncomfortable. I finished undressing and slowly laid my clothes on the sand.

"We gonna start pon de shore since you keep sayin' you can't swim. You know how me learn fe swim?" Grandad asked.

"Nope."

"Me farder chouw me in de water and he farder chouw he in de water too. None a we drown."

He told me this unbelievable story, nothing that built my confidence in the situation. Nothing that made me want to continue doing what we were doing. If this was how people learned to swim on the island, there had to be lots of bones on the ocean's floor. No way everyone survived. The only good thing I had going for me was that, luckily, we were on the shore. My insides relaxed just a little bit knowing that I could stand on the shore. That ocean? Not so much.

"Lay dung flat on you 'tomach," Grandad commanded.

I did. The water wet my face a little.

"Put you face all de way in. It's just a likkle water; it not gon kill you."

Right. I knew it didn't take much water to drown. This was a possibility too.

"Come up and breed den go dung again," Grandad instructed.

I did that several times. The water was cool and calm like it was washing the heat of the sun off my body each time I submerged my head. Each dip, my head remained longer. And longer. I did it. I wasn't swimming but I least knew how to survive underwater, like Aquaman. I was Aquaman now.

Water flooded my mouth. I coughed. More water gushed in. I couldn't breathe. Couldn't cry out for help. Was Grandad trying to kill me again? Water filled my nostrils, singed what tiny hairs I had. It felt like the salt water created its own path under my skin to get where it wanted to go and nothing was going to be able to stop it. The water leaked into my nostrils, under the skin on my face, and settled under the skin on my forehead. It burned. I didn't even know if that was biologically possible, but that was what it felt like. I struggled to stand but my feet could not find the ocean's floor. Had we moved? Were we further than where we were when we first started?

"Calm dung!" Grandad laughed. "Tan up you see you could still feel you foot."

I stood up, thanked God, and wiped the water from my face. I stood on my own two feet. Relieved, I breathed.

"Ok, less go again. Dis time a waan you lay dung pon you back. A gon hol' you."

"Please, don't let me sink, Grandad. I don't want to die." My voice shook.

"We all gon dead someday, maybe today is you day, maybe not. Eeder way you gah tu learn how to swim." No doubt Grandad knew what he was doing, knew where we were, but he said this so seriously that I didn't know whether to try to run out the ocean or just give in and die right there. But where would I go? Who would I run to?

I laid down in the water. Grandad's hands cupped my shoulders.

"Relax," he ordered.

I tried but it was so hard because yesterday I was like dead dead. I tried to forget how he tried to murder me in this very water, probably this very spot. It was so hard to close my eyes without thinking about possibly losing my life again. Every time I did, I saw Aquaman's girlfriend rescuing me. I didn't want to think about that anymore.

"Tink bout some-ting relaxing." He felt my tension.

I tried. I thought about back home: coming back from school, jumping on my Playstation, playing til my controller was drained. My friends probably missed me, especially Dunkzilla14 from California and Slay3rzay11 from New York. They probably thought I was dead or something cause I ain't logged on in so long. The sun played on my face. It wasn't burning, but felt right, like a light massage. I smiled, feeling like everything was going to be ok. The water I was floating on felt like clouds.

I didn't know how much time passed but finally Grandad joked, "Tink bout de headmaster daughter."

"What?" I said, and my relaxation sunk into the ocean. Grandad no longer held my shoulders. I struggled to find my footing on the ocean's floor. At last, I felt my feet on the soft sand. I was okay. I didn't die. He hadn't murdered me.

Grandad grinned. "See? I know you coulda swim. You just no know it."

"Grandad, that's not swimming!" I yelled.

"Not yet, but by to-marra you gon be a bara-kooda in dis sea."

Each day, Grandad picked me up from school and each day we veered from the path to the beach. We'd eat sugar cane on the way and walk behind Tess and her friends until we disappeared down that path to the beach. Sometimes other people were on the beach but barely ever. There, he taught me how to float, then doggy paddle and finally swim. I wasn't no barracuda like he said I would be, but I could get around. I even got out deep enough where I didn't need to stand. Sometimes we'd go out on the boat and now both of us would dive for the lobsters and the crab. I'd never emerge with any though cause they were still alive with their claws and biting things and I was still me. Grandad knew somebody had to stay in the boat while the other dove because the boat would swim away, so never at the same time. Boats can't even swim but I did now, is what he said. Not only did he teach me how to swim, but how to float and relax. Doing this was at times challenging cause it meant that I had to let everything go, not let things that I couldn't change consume me, not be mad at Ma, but floating helped. We were actually getting along, laughing and everything. Although I still missed Ma, I began to think things were working out just fine. Tess walked to school with me every day too. Sometimes she held my hand and sometimes she didn't, but, mostly, she did.

"You wanna go to the beach with us?" I asked one day as we walked to school.

"Wid you and you grand-farda?"

"Yeah. I mean it's right after school. You could bring your bathing suit and-"

"Me ain't know." She bit her lip.

"It's okay if you can't."

"A can. But..."

"Ok let me ask you this?" I paused for dramatic effect like I saw them do in the movies. "Where would you find an elephant?"

"What?"

"Where would you find an elephant?"

"In a zoo," she said confidently.

"Nope," I shook my head.

"African jungle?"

"Nope," I laughed. "The same place you lost her."

She laughed, "dat's stupid."

Weeks passed, so I thought she'd forgotten. This now daily occurrence of Grandad picking me up from school never failed; he was always there. After a while I just prepared myself to go to the beach after school. I'd pack my slides in my backpack for the walk home after the beach so that I wouldn't mess up my uniform shoes and socks. After the beach, I'd slip them on for the walk home, even packed the one pair of shorts that Ma had packed. I'd hang them out to dry when we got home and picked them up off the line and stuffed them in my backpack so that when Grandad picked me up, I'd be ready.

One day when Grandad came for me, Tess walked closer than usual. She didn't join Anthony and Amanda like she usually did.

"You not walking with your friends?" I asked.

At this point, I thought they were kinda like my friends too. We had all of our classes together, and we ate lunch together every day. During lunch one day, I tried one of those spicy beef patties that Anthony had been trying to get me to sample since I'd started having lunch with them. He insisted it was the best thing ever. That thing wasn't just hot from the temperature but from the heat of the spices. On its way down my throat, it burnt the skin off my tongue. I'd never tasted anything so hot in my life, like a literal volcano erupting in my mouth. "too..." I coughed, "wa,"

Amanda handed me a bottled water and I choked it down as fast as I could.

"Tek it easy, man," Anthony laughed. "Tek likkle sips,"

"Little sips?" I gasped, "this thing about to have me tongue-less,"

"I ta-rt you say you know bout dis food," Anthony laughed.

"I do," I said, "I did,"

"No worries, man, barely anybody could handle dat heat in day mout," he patted my back, "you gon be aw-right,"

"Yeah, with some more water, I'mma be aw-right," I admitted. I tried more foods after that, not spicy foods cause I wasn't gonna get caught up again, but different things like blood pudding. Sounded weird at first and looked even weirder but Anthony assured me that it wasn't like that spicy patty and he wasn't going to burn me again. He didn't. We started to grow a real bond. I don't ever remember having people like this who made me want to go to school. Sometimes, me and Anthony walked in front while the girls walked behind us talking and giggling about whatever. I even found out that Anthony had a Playstation but didn't really play that much cause he wasn't that interested. How could people not be interested in a Playstation? He was more into sports and I promised him that I would hang with him sometime and play soccer although they called it the wrong thing, football.

"You not me friend?" She answered my question with a question.

"Yeah," I said. I was. I felt like I was. I felt like she was my real friend. Nobody else really knew why I was on the island besides her and Grandad, and now Anthony and Amanda, so in a way they did feel like my real friends. Plus, ain't nobody held my hand like she did but maybe Ma when I was little. Tess holding my hand wasn't the same. It felt different than when Ma did it.

Grandad walked in front of me and Tess, but behind Anthony and Amanda, like a loner. Sill, he picked sugar cane and passed it back to me and Tess. I still wanted to break off my own piece from the field and get Tess' but didn't want a sliced hand. Somehow, I still didn't think I knew the trick to it, so I didn't even try. Grandad veered off onto the usual beach path.

"See you tomorrow, Tess?" I kinda asked but knew I was gonna see her.

"I goin' wid you today. Got me bath suit and every-ting."

"That's what's up," I said a little too excitedly.

We walked to the beach still with Grandad in front of us. Not once did he look back to check nor was he really even close enough to hear what we were saying. With Ma, she'd be all up in my business. Since I could swim now, and really swim, this wasn't gonna be too bad. Once we got to the beach, I realized that I was going to have to be almost naked in front of Tess. A bunch of thoughts of what she'd think of me filled my head. I wished I'd actually worked out, maybe stay on the track team, play some football. Anything to make me look like what I didn't.

"Das how you does go in de war-ta?" Tess asked.

"Naw" I answered. Slowly, I picked at each button on my shirt like I'd never unbuttoned a shirt before. I looked over at Grandad who was busy paying me no mind. I left my unbuttoned shirt on and worked on my shoes. The sand covered my naked feet as they sank. Tess undressed too, like I wasn't right in front of her with my two widely opened eyes. She unbuckled her belt from her skirt and pulled her shirt from her waist. Then she unbuttoned her uniform shirt. Everything seemed to be moving in slow motion. She dropped her uniform skirt on the sand and stepped out of it. I swallowed hard, loud enough to think that maybe she and Grandad heard me swallowing. I'd seen plenty of girls in next to nothing before. I mean, I lived in Spring Break Central. Plus, those girls in Orlando barely wore clothes to school, never mind the beach. I sometimes wondered if they weren't cold in class cause I mostly wore a hoodie. But this felt different. This wasn't my first time undressing but this was my first time undressing in front of a girl, in front of Tess. And, this was the first time a girl was undressing in front of me.

"Kadeem?" Grandad called. "Come help me wid dis boat."

Grandad never needed help before. Plus, how was I gonna help him. I walked over to him anyway. "Yes, Grandad?"

"You just over a day a watch de gyal hard." He shook his head.

"I wasn't staring, Grandad." I sought of whispered hoping that Tess wouldn't hear.

"Ok, and goat no got no tail."

He was right. I was staring. I tried to lighten things up a bit. "Grandad, where would you find an elephant?"

"Oh, lawd." I turned. Tess wore a two-piece black bathing suit with a small gold rectangle on each side of her hips. Faint, fine hairs curled under her navel, not enough to look gross but enough to notice. She had an innie belly button that looked like it hid from everything and everybody. I swallowed hard again.

"Wa I looking fa a elephant fa?" Grandad asked.

"It's a joke, Grandad," I said playfully.

"Looking fa a elephant is a joke?" Grandad asked. "Dat doan mek no sense. Strupes." He sucked his teeth, jumped in his boat, rowed away and left me there with Tess and her black two-piece bathing suit.

CHAPTER 14

Everything was going great. Grades weren't just good; they were all A's, even in that stupid English class. Writing one more essay was probably gonna transform me into a book, but I didn't complain. I wrote the papers, counted the numbers, even volunteered to answer questions. I did the work. I was getting along with everybody, not getting into trouble. Maybe the daily cool breeze from the ocean or the lack of hallways made things easy going here. *Irie*, like the Rastas say. Nobody was sweating me bout nothing. Me and Grandad was having good times, lots of good times. Probably, I was gonna start turning into a sea creature though, one with claws and fins cause we ate something from the sea almost every day: crabs, lobsters, wilks, snapper, king fish, all sorts of things. I couldn't remember the last time I had chicken or even steak. The Chik Fila cows would be pleased. Grandad hardly used his stove. He cooked outside in the backyard, using a coal pot. He made everything so simple and mostly fun. Maybe this was like camping - cooking outside at night, sitting on an upside-down bucket and eating. Definitely different from Ma bringing home takeout when she was tired.

Yeah, sometimes Grandad acted crazy but when I really thought about it, he mostly made sense. Like a couple of times he took me to play soccer. Well, Grandad and everybody else on the island called it football, so okay, football. Anyway, on those occasions that he took me to play football, he'd always take off his shoes. Me? I just watched him from the sidelines. I didn't have no cleats. I wondered if his feet didn't hurt kicking the ball or even just being barefooted. When I ran track, I had shoes specifically for track. Shoot, I had shoes specifically for everything that I did. I could never imagine being barefooted doing nothing, especially running on the dirt ground with my bare feet. He didn't look like anything hurt when he kicked that ball then ran behind it to kick it some more. When I finally asked Grandad why he gonna kick the ball without shoes, he would always say, "Why me gon' mess up me good shoes pon dis ball in a dis dut." I guessed he made sense, but I sometimes wondered if his feet didn't hurt from the hard ground or little pebbles. No nice green grass or even sand, but hard and dirty ground without cleats, I just didn't get it.

Grandad, as always, moved around the soccer field like he was just as young as the other players. His body moved smoothly to kick the ball in whatever direction he aimed. At times, he even head-butted the ball in a particular direction. That was wild to me! He never stopped even once to catch his breath or let someone sub for him. On the rare occasions that he made a goal, oh man. We'd talk about that the entire walk home. "Boy, you see me mek dat goal! Nobody coulda touch me!" His eyes would sparkle. Meanwhile, he kicked a ball with his bare feet on a dusty ball field. His feet were so dirty, I could just imagine him sitting down for a pedicure.

"Grandad!" I'd tell him. "We gonna have to get you a pedicure when we go back to Orlando."

"Not me," he'd say. "Nobody a go touch me foot dem."

I'd laugh cause I was sure that nobody wanted to touch his feet, not after he was baking them in the dirt.

I didn't mind waking up early on Saturdays to go to the mountains, to garden, then to town for the market. That was a regular trip for me now. Sometimes I'd even see Tess with her parents, Mr. and Mrs. Headmaster, shopping in the market too. Seeing Tess was always a treat. Sometimes I even woke up before Grandad. Naw, not really. I ain't never been able to wake up before him; that was definitely too out-a-pocket. I'm not sure he even slept, not like a normal old human being anyway. He had so much energy with that daily walk from school. He never used one of his two vans or even just let me walk home alone with Tess and my friends.

I was doing good. Why should he and Ma worry about me? Ma, she called a lot more, probably cause I stopped begging her to come get me. I'd tell her about some of the crazy things Grandad did, but nothing seemed like a surprise to her. She said she used to go to the mountain to garden too. I couldn't picture that at all. I couldn't picture Ma's hand in dirt digging out no weeds but she said she had to do it, every Saturday morning, rain or shine.

Sometimes Grandad even let me drive one of the vans, of course the older one. I was afraid at first cause I didn't want to get pulled over by the police, but Grandad would say, "Bwoy, doan bodda dem and day naw go bodda you." Sometimes I drove to the market. I only accidentally drove off the road once, maybe twice, I was definitely a better driver for sure. Sometimes I wondered if Grandad ever followed rules or did he just make his own as he went through life. Cause me, it was only a couple fights for Ma to drop me here. But I wasn't complaining no more. I was liking it... loving it, actually. And Tess, she was amazing. Why didn't Ma send me to school here sooner?

All my classes were going great. My band class wasn't at all what I expected. It was probably the only class that we could really move around in when the teacher was in the room. Band was one of the only times we left the classroom except for lunch and the end of school. Located in the building on the hill above the front office, it was not the kind of band that I expected. We learned how to play steel pan music. I'd heard it before but to actually learn how to play was another thing. This teacher was young too. Some of the kids said that he played in a local band so that's why his class was actually fun. Before class, he'd have the radio playing a song we were gonna practice. Tess said they did this every year, learned the music to play in the upcoming Carnival. I'd been to Carnival before because Ma's got pics of me with the masquerades but I couldn't remember. So, I was starting to look forward to it - playing in the band, actually being a part of Carnival.

Tess stood in front of me in class. I played the bass pans in the back of the room. Very few people were assigned to them, probably because there weren't that many. The bass drums were tall drums that one player was in charge of. I stood in the middle of four big barreled drums, so all I basically had to know was when to pound each one. If I listened carefully to the beat and *felt* it like the teacher said, he didn't have to call me much to remind me to hit the pan. Tess? She was right up front on the single pan, the one that carried all the melody. That single pan was the hardest one to learn, too, because even though there were tons of numbers inside the pan to help, when to hit what, where and when, to play and have fun with it, players had to know them numbers by heart. Tess always joked that without her, the band wouldn't have no melody. She'd dance a little when she said this, moving her waistline to the music she heard in her head. She was right, though; her section carried all the melody. All I did was make a sound once in a while; no one would miss that at all. But in true Tess fashion, when I did say stuff like that, she'd make me feel like the band wasn't nothing without my section. We both knew that wasn't true, but she still made me feel important.

After school was always beach time which, with band and Tess, made school so much easier to handle. Tess went with me and Grandad, too, most days. The black two piece made way to all sorts of colored bathing suits, some just one shoulder and floral. She hardly wore the same bathing suit twice, but in each one, she looked like a cold red Gatorade on an Orlando summer day. She looked gooood. What made her even prettier is that she didn't even act like she knew how pretty she was. Even better, she laughed at every joke I told, even the ones I destroyed because I was laughing too hard. Grandad would say when Tess couldn't hear him, "Dat gyal must like you cause only deaf people a go laugh at you joke dem."

One day after school, Grandad wasn't at the gate like he usually was in his normal, not-so-swag clothes. Tess, Anthony and Amanda still walked home, no worries. I walked with them on the normal route like the rest of the kids. I thought and thought about still going to the beach. I thought about maybe putting it off since Grandad wasn't there. To be honest, he wasn't really there any way cause he didn't pay us much attention. This wasn't really gonna be any different. Finally, I decided to go without him and pray that this was one of the times that Tess would come too.

"You goin' beach still?" she asked before I could.

"Yeah," I tried to break off a piece of sugar cane like I knew what I was doing. "I mean, if you still want to, not sure what Grandad has planned for us."

"Yeah, we can go if you no fraid me." She laughed.

"No, you're harmless." I laughed nervously. But was I?

We veered off the path like we normally did with Grandad, the two of us silent as we walked. She didn't try to hold my hand, so I didn't try to hold hers. I was starting to think that maybe we should've just walked home and not gone to the beach, but it was too late cause we were already on the shore looking out far onto the ocean with our backs to the land. The breeze was high, blowing our uniforms against our skins. We heard nothing but the ocean breeze and the waves crashing against the seashore. Tess dropped her book-bag on the sand and started to undress. Even though I knew she wasn't actually moving in slow motion, it again looked like she was. Why was this, though? It was like time slowed down for us. I liked the slow and peaceful pace that seemed to surround her. I liked her. She slowly pulled her shirt from her skirt's waist. Then she slowly unbuttoned each button. I hadn't realized it before, but although our uniform shirts were the same, hers seem to have more buttons or maybe it was all in my mind. This time, she wore a white one-piece bathing suit. A large brownish orange flower with petals covered part of her back and part of her stomach. Relief swept over me cause I didn't have to stare at her bare stomach with those little curled-up hairs. Grandad had taught me a trick, though. Focus on something less exciting like food or something like that. Unfortunately, food made me excited too. Anyway, I tried not to pay attention to her especially since she was so quiet. Then, she took her hair out of the wrapped up ponytail that she always wore. It was so long. The wind carried her hair away from her face like in a photo shoot or something and the photographer blew a fan in front of her just for her hair. For me, Grandad had already ruined my-hair-blowing-in-the-wind chances. I sat on the beach, digging my toes into the sand. She tucked in right next to me, so close that I could smell her hair.

Both of us stared out far into the ocean for some time and I couldn't help to wonder if Ma was right to send me here. I knew she had her reasons. Well, reason. I'd had so much time to really think about some of those things that I'd done. So many things I could've avoided. So many better choices I could've made. I hated that it took this, Ma's anger to get me to realize it. But, she was right, this was what I needed. I'd been pissed at first especially with the way that she'd basically dragged me out of the house with no idea of where we were going. But I'd never had this before - the ability to just sit, watch, and enjoy. Peace. Walking to the beach each day allowed that. Hanging with Grandad allowed that. Being with Tess definitely allowed that.

"Is that mint in your hair?" I asked awkwardly.

"Yeah," she ran her hand through her hair. "You like it?"

"It's ok, I guess."

"You guess?"

"I mean, it's alright for shampoo." Omg. Were we having a lame conversation about shampoo? "I just didn't imagine someone using mint for shampoo. Grandad and Ma use mint for tea so I just thought it was used only for food." I babbled.

"Yeah, you can use it for whatever you want. I actually does mek me own shampoo wid aloes, mint, and water. It 'pose to make me hair longer and stronger." She moved closer to me leaving nothing between us. "Feel it."

I did. I looped some of it around my fingers. It was soft and long. "It's strong, all right, and it's definitely long."

"Tanks!" She was so close to me that now our legs touched. My hairy legs looked like dead monsters next to her smooth skin.

"So..." I said.

"Stitch."

"Stitch?"

"Yea, you said *so,* so I said *stitch.*"

"Oh, ok." I didn't get it but she laughed so I smiled too.

"So, what's goin' on wid you? You gonna stay a wa?"

"Looks like I'm staying."

"It won't be that bad, promise."

"Naw, it's ok."

"Ok?" She faked gasped. "So, you have all dis in Orlando? Beach every day? Fresh air? A girlfriend with strong, long hair?"

Wait! What?

"You naw kiss me less I kiss you?"

"Um..."

And just like that, she leaned over, her lips were touching mines, kissing me. And I was kissing her back. And Ma could keep her Chik Fila sauce all to herself. And I was glad Grandad wasn't here. And St. Kitts wasn't too bad. And I was glad I was staying. And... and...

CHAPTER 15

A nd...
   The walk home from the beach was much stranger than usual. Yeah, by now I was used to Tess holding my hand, but her hand felt softer now. And my hand felt softer. Both our hands felt like they should melt together, clinging to each other until they weren't. This was the first time I'd walked her to her gate. Everything seemed more visible, like when you first test an Impossible Whopper. You know it's not real meat so you kind of expect it not to taste so good, but then after a bite, it actually tastes really really good, so good you can't believe that it's not real meat. This was like that, like I really had a girlfriend, a real girlfriend.

"I think Ma would like you," I stated.

"Yeah?" She hooked her arm in mine without letting go of my hand. "Why you say dat?"

"I don't know," I shrugged my shoulders, "she just would."

"A mean, who wouldn't?"

"True."

From the top of the road, we walked through a narrow alley to stop at the first gate on the left. She clung to me even tighter. The fence was similar to Grandad's: a smaller gate for us to walk through and a larger gate for a vehicle. I didn't notice it before, but most of the houses had the same setup. Must be an island thing.

She opened the smaller gate, her arm loosening because I wasn't yet moving.

"You naw come in?"

"Naw, I'm good."

"Really?" She asked. "Wa mek?"

"It's late," I lied. Grandad would say that we had plenty of day left, but I didn't want to go into her house. No telling what was going to happen. Even though she said she was my girlfriend, she still had parents in that house, or on their way home at least. Her dad was still the principal or headmaster, whatever they called him here. Ma always warned me: "Do not go into a girl's house without her parent's invitation." Not that I had tons of invites, but that was always something that stuck with me.

"Ok, den," she tiptoed and moved her face closer to mine. Yes, I wanted her to continue kissing me. I wanted to continue kissing her, but we were in front of her house, in front of inquiring eyes. I squeezed my eyes shut anyway waiting for her lips to land on mine. "Boop," I opened my eyes and she smiled, not in a I-got-you kinda way but in a playful kinda way.

"You play too much," I griped.

"Yeah," she closed the gate, using the fence to separate us. "See you to-marra, Kadeem!"

"See you tomorrow, Tess," I stood there and watched her walk into her house flashing back to how Ma used to watch me walk all the way into the school when I was a little kid, projecting her affection around me like a protective bubble.

The walk home was easy and short. By now, I knew exactly which shortcuts to take and through whose yards to walk. There were players on the soccer field kicking a ball when I passed by. Some were barefooted like Grandad, running on the dirt and smacking that ball like they had second mysterious layers of skin, but Grandad wasn't there with them. He wasn't giving them a run for their money. I wondered that if when Grandad saw me, could he tell that I was different? He probably would. He was probably gonna say, *you a big man now wid gyal and ting*. I couldn't wait to tell him what Tessa said. I smiled. With Grandad, he probably already knew.

Both vehicles were in the yard when I got home. *Home*. Weird sounding, I was home now. Ma wasn't coming back for me, not til the end of the school year anyway, so this really was my home. Just like Tess said, I was going to make the best of it and she was gonna help me. Grandad wasn't so bad, but now Tess added a new layer of comfort to this home.

Maybe we were going to have some non-ocean food for dinner since Grandad hadn't gone to the beach today. Definitely I felt like fins were growing somewhere on my body. I was gonna be able to race Aquaman soon! Calypso music blared through his open windows: either Grandad was in the back cooking on his coal pot or washing clothes.

"Grandad," I yelled!

He wasn't in the backyard but the backdoor was open, the breeze blew the curtain in and out of the doorway like a big leaf. From the radio came that real old Calypso that told a full-blown story in slow motion, not the fast rhythm calypso that we listened to in steel pan class - *real music* Grand called it, not that mess we listen to he'd say. I couldn't imagine Tess dancing to this. I couldn't imagine anybody dancing to this stuff. I turned off the music.

"Grandad," I yelled again.

No answer.

I knocked on his closed door. Man, I'd never been in Grandad's room, not once since I'd been here. I turned the knob slowly hoping that I wasn't intruding. Me and Ma had unspoken rules: we knocked, waited, then entered. I would never just walk into Ma's room and she would never just walk into mine neither. I opened the door slowly and peeked in.

"Grandad?" I whispered. "You in here?"

The large TV mounted on the wall, Netflix asking if Grandad was still watching. Meanwhile, there was no TV in my room, and I wasn't even sure if the one in the living room worked since Grandad had a huge plant on top of it and he never turned it on. But this whole time he had been in here watching Netflix on his big screen TV like I didn't like Netflix too? The only thing missing was a sweet video game hook-up. A bed large enough to fit Grandad at least four times sat in the middle of the room, way more space than he needed and two night stands on either side. One night stand held a lamp but instead of a lampshade, crowned a mountain of every color straw hat. Grandad's room was neat and clean, not a thing out of place. On his dresser stood several bottles of cologne, weird cause Grandad always smelled of seawater and coal pot smoke. His closet door was wide open. Several business suits hung neatly pressed. How many suits did one man need? Several pairs of more stylish sandals sat on the floor of the closet. Other items were folded on shelves in color coordinating fashion. Guess he couldn't wear this stuff to pick me up since we were always going to the beach after school. But, dang, he had a lot of clothes. I may have to rethink taking his swag card.

I saw the remote on the top of the nightstand on the other side of his bedroom. I walked around to get it so I could at least catch up on some of my shows while he was out. I was certain that he wouldn't mind.

Oh, my God - NO!

Grandad laid face down on the floor!

"Grandad?" I whispered, not processing what I saw. Was he doing some type of crazy yoga routine or something? It wouldn't surprise me if he was. Still, he didn't move.

"Grandad?" I bent to tap him on his shoulder.

Nothing.

"Grandad?" I shook him, but still nothing. Some sort of white foam leaked from his mouth to the carpet.

"Grandad!" I shouted, my heart raced fast and loud; surely the pounding would wake him up!

"Grandaaad!"

"Ugh," he finally grunted.

"Jesus, Grandad, what happened?" I put both arms around him to help him sit up.

"Ugh," he barely breathed.

"You alright, Grandad?" I looked around searching for his phone so I could call 911. "Where's your phone, Grandad, I gotta call 911. We gotta get help."

"Ah, ah," he mumbled. "No na wa..."

"I gotta get you to the hospital, Grandad," I said fiercely.

"Ah, ah," he shook his head no, "no na wa.."

"What?" I put my ear closer to his lips so I could hear what he was mumbling.

"Ke," he tried to lift his finger to point, but it fell limply to his side as he slouched. "Ke, you gah tu tek me,"

"Me? How, Grandad? We gotta call the ambulance," I protested.

"Ah, ah," he weakly shook his head again.

I could do this. I forced my feet to move, draping his arm over my shoulder, supporting his entire body. Grandad's body felt light like I'd suddenly grown much needed muscles. I moved as quickly as I could and carefully placed him in the passenger side of the older and bigger van cause that was the one closer to the gate. I ran back in the house, got the keys and ran back out. I opened the gate and backed out easily.

"Grandad, I don't know where the hospital is," I admitted.

"Go lak," he sighed, "lak you a go a mar-kit."

I drove the same way as we would to go to the market, like he said. It was a good thing that he was having me drive to the market on Saturdays, so much so that the directions were as familiar to me as the beach. I just didn't remember ever seeing a hospital no place close to the market. Where could it be? I drove trying not to veer off the road. That's when Grandad passed out again.

"Grandad, stay with me." His eyelids barely lifted as he slouched in the seat. Vehicles whipped around us cause I was driving the speed limit; no one else but me ever drove the speed limit on this island. Everyone seemed to be in a hurry when they were driving. Walking and beach life were totally different, I guessed. Then, time didn't matter. But it mattered now!

"Tun on you lights," one driver screamed out his vehicle as he passed us. I did.

"Grandad," I tapped him lightly. "We're coming up on the market."

"Ugh," he groaned.

"I don't know where to go," I confessed.

"Tun up day so," he barely lifted his hand to point to an alley that was next to the market.

I did. The alley looked as though it had barely enough room for the van to go through. Other cars wedged alongside, making the alley even narrower. I tried my best not to hit the other cars. Miraculously, I didn't. At the end of the alley was a sprawling one-story building sitting on top of a hill. If **JN France General Hospital** wasn't in bold letters on the front of the building, I would have dismissed it as a really big house. I followed the driveway around to the entrance of the building and stopped the van right in front of the entrance.

"Grandad, they got ambulances here," I pointed out. There were several ambulances parked on the side of the building.

"Ah ah, no na wan.." he reached for the door handle.

"I got you, Grandad." I ran around to his side to help him. I draped his arm over my shoulder. This was not the ER I knew! Where were the security guard and wheelchairs out front? Seriously? Where was everybody? It was the *Walking Dead* again. With Grandad heavily draped over me, I pulled the door open.

"You need help?" a man in a black uniform asked.

"Yes, please," I begged

"Is wa happen to him?" he lifted Grandad's other arm and draped it over his shoulder so that he could help me. Lights came on in the building as we walked.

"I don't know," I said.

Two women in white dresses and white hats ran out from another hallway frantically asking questions that I had no answers to.

"What happened to him?" Her accent was deep like Grandad's but, thankfully, clear.

"I don't know," I answered.

"Sir?" The other asked. They must've been nurses cause nobody else was coming out to help us. In fact, was anyone else even here? "Can you hear me?"

"Eh," Grandad barely answered.

"Can you tell me why you are here?"

"I found him lying on the ground, face down," I admitted.

"No, he has to tell us," the lady said, like what I said didn't matter. She looked at Grandad. "Sir?"

"White stuff was coming from his mouth when I found him." I ignored her, "he couldn't even walk to the car."

"Is you drive here?" the guy in the black uniform asked suspiciously.

Grandad groaned and lost his grip around my neck. The other lady ran out with a wheelchair and helped Grandad to sit in it.

"What medications are you on?" she asked as she rolled him down the hallway.

"He's not on anything," I followed, "I don't think."

They rolled him into an empty room with a high skinny bed. No way was Grandad going to be able to sit on top of this high thing. The lady wrapped his arm with that cuff thing while Grandad stayed in the wheelchair. I was glad that she let him sit cause even Grandad could barely sit up. She squeezed, pumping air into the cuff wrapped around Grandad's arm. "One eighty over..." she mumbled.

"What does that mean?"

"A soon come," she said and left me with Grandad.

The room seemed smaller than it actually was. The pure white walls held little pictures of palm trees. I kept trying to help Grandad to sit up straight because he kept slouching down.

"Grandad, you tired?"

He shook his head *yes*.

"What happened?"

He shook his head *yes*.

"How come you got Netflix and you ain't even let me know?"

His lips curved into a smile.

"We have to admit him," the lady said rushing back into the room. Her accent was thick but clear. She took the brakes off the chair and started to push Grandad out the room.

"Ah, ah," Grandad protested.

"Grandad, you have to listen to them. You gotta do what they say! Do you know what's wrong with him?" I followed her.

"We have to run some tests..." she stopped the wheelchair and looked me up and down, "you no got nobody else older dan you?"

"Yes," I lied. "Ma's at work."

"Ok, when she comes, I gonna give a de infa-mation," her accent changed back and forth as she spoke to me.

"Where are you taking him?"

"Mmmm," Grandad moaned.

"We tekking him to a room to watch til he pressure go dung," she stated.

I followed them down the hallway that seemed to never end.

"You can't stay wid him eh," she corrected.

"But, I have to," I protested, "I have to!"

CHAPTER 16

"Kadeeeem,"

I heard her voice even in my dreams. We must've been on the beach again, but I couldn't see her. I only heard, "Kadeeeeem," like she was yelling my name.

"Kadeeem," she yelled again, but I still couldn't see her. All I saw were angry waves crashing against the shoreline, tall walls of blues and grays falling to the sand, then forming a white foamy mess on the shore that dragged itself back to the ocean to start again. The waves shook the anchored boats out of place, each one disappearing under a large wave. I wanted to save them, tie them back so the waves wouldn't drag them out to sea and destroy them, but my feet wouldn't move. The more I tried to move them, the deeper they sunk into the sand. Energy seeped out my body leaving me weak. I was frantic, unable to save not even myself. The sand was winning. With my feet swallowed by the sand, I fell to the ground and watched helplessly as the mighty waves angrily gulped each boat.

I opened my eyes slowly. The chicken outside my window still hadn't made a sound and Grandad wasn't outside, making a ruckus for no reason.

"Kadeeem," sounded like it came from my window but how, when I was still dreaming? "you in day?"

"Yeah," I answered.

"You naw go a school?"

"Yeah." Dang, what time was it? I unlocked all four locks from the front door. The sun was bright like it had been out there for a long time. Tess wore her uniform, neatly pressed pleated green skirt and khaki collared shirt. She was always on point with her uniform, just like the rest of the kids at that school. She walked into the house and stood still at the door.

"You naw go a school?" she asked again.

"Yeah," I said rubbing my eyes open. "I'm going."

"Well, you no dress and school start long time."

"What time is it?"

"Past ten," she said. "How you just here? No uniform? You no know we got school today?"

"What?" I headed for my bedroom looking for my uniform.

"Yeah," she didn't move from the door. "You done miss a couple a classes eh."

I quickly put on my uniform, grabbed my backpack and met her back in the living room. My uniform was in no way as neat as hers as it had been balled up in my backpack since last night. I didn't have a chance to wash it or hang it.

"What happens when you're late there?"

"Happen like wa?"

"When you get to school late," I repeated. "What happens to you?"

"Nuttin'."

"Nothing?" That sounded strange. In Orlando, we got a warning, then in-school detention, then eventually out of school suspension. I knew this because I was late often enough to earn every single one of these consequences.

"Way you gran-fard-a?"

"The hospital." Time stopped for a moment and I forgot what I was doing and where I was going. Grandad was in the hospital where I'd left him the night before.

"Hospital?" She sounded unsure. "Fuh wa?"

"Let's go through the back door," I suggested.

"Yeah, ok," she followed me thorough the back door so that we could leave for school. "Why he in de hospital?"

"No idea, Tess." I could feel the inside of my head starting to burn with a headache.

"Wat you mean *no idea*?" she grilled. "He gone see somebody? He gone carry somebody? Some-ting wrong wid him?"

"I don't know, Tess." I really didn't know. "I found him on the floor when I got home yesterday. At first I thought he was just lying there but then he didn't respond."

"Oh," she frowned.

"I tried to wake him but he didn't move,"

"How he get to de hospital cause me no hear no siren?"

"I drove him," I confessed.

"From when you get you license to drive here?"

"I don't have one, but Grandad didn't want me to call the ambulance."

"Well, day expensive, nobody don't really call dem less day want to dead and dead poor."

"Do you think we can skip school and go there instead?"

"Naw. We can't do that," she said apprehensively.

"You don't have to," I said maybe a little too angrily.

"It's not that."

"Really?" It wasn't even worth begging her to go any place with me. I got Grandad there on my own, and I would get to him on my own too. Plus, I didn't want her to think that she had to miss the rest of school just for me. "Really, it's fine. I can get there. I'll just have to miss school today."

"Kadeem, day not gon' let you in."

"What? That's crazy," I complained. "I need to check on Grandad. He was a mess when I left last night."

"First off, it's de middle of de day, day naw go let no chile' in de hospital when day 'pose to day a school."

"But..."

"And second," she added, "day naw go lay you in by you-self. You no ol' enough."

"That's B.S.!" I shouted. "In Orlando...,"

"You Grand-farda ain't in Orlando, Kadeem."

She was right. Things were certainly different here and I needed to be reminded of that. I still hadn't told Ma what was going on, not that I thought she was going to do anything or could even do anything. But, maybe she needed to at least know what was up. I couldn't imagine anything like this happening to Ma. Telling her would probably only worry her even more. She and Grandad was tight, especially since he was the only parent she had. Naw, she wasn't gonna be good with this at all.

"Les' just go to school, Kadeem and we can..."

"Naw, I'm not going." Though we had already walked through the gate, I spun around."Kadeem," her voice was soft, "trust me eh, day not gon' lay you in. The best ting fuh you to do is to go to school. A gon' talk to daddy and see wa he could do."

"What could your father do?"

"Way more dan you," she said confidently. What could her father really do? We weren't family so they definitely weren't going to allow him to even see Grandad. My head started to hurt again just thinking about what could possibly happen. This was good, better than any plan I had. If Tess' dad could get me into the hospital, I could check on Grandad and make sure that he was okay. Make sure that he had everything he needed. Make sure he'd be home soon.

We entered school just at the end of lunch and just like she said, no one asked any questions or even acted as though they knew we were late. The teachers came to the classroom, taught and left. The day dragged on and seemed like it would never end. None of the classes mattered, not even band could break my haze.

We were in English class when the headmaster walked in. He whispered something to the woman with the narrow belt and buttoned-down collared dress. I pictured her at the door to her closet facing rows of identical outfits.

"Tess and Kadeem," the headmaster announced, "come with me."

Here it was, the punishment for not showing up for morning classes. I was doing so well, not getting in trouble, staying out of people's way, no fights. Whatever consequence he'd give us for being late would be worth it. Grandad was the only thing on my mind. I got up to follow him.

"Grab you bag," Tess commanded.

"Why?" I asked. "We're not coming back?"

"Me no know, but me doan' leave me bag way me no day."

She was right as usual. It made no sense for me to leave my bag where I wasn't. Carrying our bag packs, we followed the headmaster down to the front office. This was all too familiar. Administrators didn't come for me unless I was in trouble, unless they were writing me up. Now, *we* were in trouble cause he came for both of us. Tess had said nothing happened to tardies, but they got us even before school was out! We followed straight into his office. I guessed that Tess was wrong. But, it didn't even matter. I hadn't done anything wrong. I'd made practically good decisions since being here, Grandad's standards anyway. I was different and I knew it. Whatever consequences came with being late would be fine, just tell me how you can help me get to Grandad.

"I just heard about your grandfather." He picked up a briefcase from his desk and walked back towards us as though he were heading back through the door. "We will go to him now," he stated flatly.

This was good. More than good. He was gonna take me to Grandad. This was all that mattered.

"Ok," I said, guardedly. Tess was right again! She said her dad would take care of it and he did. We followed him to a smaller van than Grandad's smallest van, and without words, got in. Tess rode shotgun, and I moved the soccer ball and cleats out of the way so I could sit in the back. Guess headmaster didn't play barefooted like Grandad. I smiled. We had to get Grandad back playing on the field, barefoot or not.

Headmaster drove just like everyone else on the island, as if every place was far away and time was fleeting. Buildings, houses, markets closed in on each other, so why drive so fast? Plus, the roads were narrow and seemingly dangerous. Nonetheless, I grabbed the handle in the roof so tightly that my knuckles bulged.

"How long has your grand-fartha been ill?" the headmaster finally asked.

"Huh?"

"Not well," he repeated. "Sick. How long has he been sick?"

"Since yesterday," I guessed. "I don't know."

I told him what I told Tess about finding Grandad on the floor. Talking about it didn't make it seem real cause I still couldn't imagine Grandad motionless, never mind in a hospital bed. Was it a movie? Did it even happen? What did I know? I didn't know how long he had been there. I didn't know what he was suffering from. All I knew is that he wasn't there to walk me home from school like he usually was and when I found him, he didn't look like *my* Grandad. In fact, he looked older, not like someone who played soccer barefooted and dove for our dinner.

"I am certain he is fine," the headmaster said, but he seemed unsure as he glanced at me in the mirror.

"I'm sure he is, too," I agreed, really wanting to believe those words. "Whatever is going on, me and Grandad will handle it together." That I believed. I believed that whatever was going on with him, I'd do whatever it took to make sure that he was *my* Grandad again.

The headmaster parked his small van in an empty space in the parking lot. He had his choices, there were a lot of empty spots in the parking lot. Were not a lot of people sick or were a lot of people sick but just didn't have visitors? We walked up to the door, same entrance as the night before, but this time there were people at the front, a security guard like last night, an actual nurse at the front desk. The headmaster mumbled something to her. She looked at us, shook her head and mumbled something back at the headmaster.

"It's ok," Mr. Turnbull said to Tess, "we soon come."

"I'm fine," I said, "I can go in by myself."

"No," Tess shook her head, "day doan lay young people in by dem-self."

I rolled my eyes, another rule that made absolutely no sense. I wasn't a little kid. I was practically raising myself! Except for

Grandad making my breakfast and dinner, I was actually a man - an almost-man. If I could drive Grandad here, I was definitely old enough to see him by myself. But, I didn't say that. I didn't complain, I just followed the headmaster down the same corridor they made me leave the night before.

There were several beds in the room and one other patient. The room looked like something you'd see in an army movie, with a bunch of single beds. The only difference were curtains that could be pulled across to separate the patients. Grandad laid curled up in one of the narrow beds, his back turned towards the door. His body looked small, like he'd shrunk from last night to now.

"Ol' man," Tess' dad said a little too loudly, "is wa goin on?"

"Eh, man," his voice was weak.

"I hear you up here givin' some trouble."

"Naw, man," the sound of Grandad's voice barely left his mouth. "Dis body here naw car-pa-rate t'all."

Grandad looked tired, weak even, like he had played a hundred games of soccer. I wanted to say something to him, but what? Dang, I didn't even know what to say. *Hey, Grandad, what you up to?* Naw. *Grandad, what's good?* All these thoughts in my head of how to approach him. *Can I do anything for you?* Nothing seemed right to say in the moment. What do you say to your Grandad who's laid up in the hospital? What?

"Kadeem?" Grandad peeked. He looked like he struggled to see me, maybe because I hadn't really moved from the doorway.

"Yes, Grandad," my voice was low since this was a hospital where we could potentially disturb other patients.

"Come closer, no?"

I did. I took one step closer to him, still out of reach though he stretched his arm towards me.

"Bwoy, come over 'ere now, mek me see you good," Grandad commanded.

I moved closer. If I compared the number of wrinkles he had before and the number of wrinkles I saw now, no question that he had more now. His skin drooped below his eyes, farther it seemed than before. This wasn't my walk-home-from-school-to-the-beach-every-day Grandad.

"Is wa you cryin' fa?"

I hadn't realized, but tears spilled from my eyes down my chin.

"He gon' be aw-right, man." Headmaster Turnbull patted me on the back.

"Nothing," I said, wiping the tears. "Nothing."

CHAPTER 17

"Kadeem, I don't have time for your games," Ma said.

"I ain't playing, Ma," I was serious, as serious as the Wifi going out just before I won a game. The thing was that she spoke to me like this was one of the other times I had called her to beg her to come get me. It wasn't. Had she even realized I hadn't done that in months? In fact, I hadn't spoken to her for some time now. I missed her, but after a while I saw what she was doing, not *to* me but *for* me and, after that, I didn't miss her so much anymore; I just understood. Talks with Grandad did that, opened my mind to what I really didn't see or maybe couldn't see.

One night Grandad said to me, "Man naw go win no war God no sen' 'em to fight."

We were sitting outside around the coal pot cracking shells off of lobsters and crabs and eating the meat. Very few mosquitoes buzzed around us. I only had to brush off a few. It was a habit now for us: beach after school, catch lobster or crab or lobster and crab, then home to cook them. Sometimes we'd catch wilks too, another type of shell fish, but whatever we caught, was gonna be dinner - mostly lobster or crab or lobster and crab. I didn't even need that little hammer Red Lobster provided to crack the shells anymore. I learned to crack them with my bare hands and suck the meat right from the shells like Grandad. Surely, Ma wasn't gonna like my slurping sound when she eventually heard me. But Grandad didn't say nothing about it cause he made that same sound too.

"What that mean, Grandad?" I asked, "Why you don't just say what you mean so I don't have to guess all of the time?"

"Who mek you fight all dem fight you fight?" he asked in between the sounds of cracking and sucking, "dem fights in school?"

"People be trying me, Grandad," I confessed. Just because I look small, they think I won't do nothing. "They be trying to punk me."

"Punk you? Wat dat mean?"

"Make me feel like I'm not a man?"

"A man?" He spat out some pieces of lobster which landed in the grass. "Is wa mek you a man?"

I had no answer. I thought about his words for a long time that night, and I couldn't come up with an answer to save my life. Why did I get in to those fights? Why couldn't I just walk away?

Anyway, Ma acted like this was one of those phone calls. It wasn't. I wasn't trying to go home, not this time. Not that I didn't want to go back home at all, but I'd lost interest in begging her and getting nowhere. The island had already made itself my home and I was fine with that. I annoyed myself with all my asking, so I couldn't even begin to imagine how Ma was feeling about it. Sometimes she didn't even answer the phone when I called. Besides, things were actually going good here. I meant really, really good. I wasn't getting in no trouble. I hadn't been suspended, not one time. Not even close to being suspended. By now, in Orlando, I would've at least been in one or two fights and on my way to an expulsion meeting. It was so easy going here. No one stepped on anyone's new J's, probably cause we all wore the same style shoes as part of our uniform - not J's, by the way. No one pushed anyone in the hallway if they wanted space. Plus, there wasn't no hallway here. If someone really wanted to, they could just push a person over the railing, but it never happened. People just went about their business like nothing bothered nobody for no reason. People weren't fake super nice here, but they weren't not nice either. *Not-nice* was all right with me. Why hadn't I noticed this before? This was my home. Here, on the island, where everything made sense. Where everything was as it should be.

"Okay," she sighed, "Tell me what's going on."

I told her the same story I told Tess and her father: finding Grandad with his face down, foam coming out of his mouth, him not moving. I did not tell her that I drove Grandad to the hospital on the narrow streets of St. Kitts because I still didn't want her to worry about my driving and why he was letting me drive without a license. That was something we would talk about later, if it ever came up. Her eyes opened wider and wider as I told her each part of the story.

"Where is Daddy now?" she asked.

"In the hospital," I said.

"How long?"

"Just a couple of days," I assured her.

"What's a couple of days, Kadeem?"

"About a week, Ma," I said.

"Is it *about* a week or an actual week?" she asked. "Which is it?"

"A week, Ma."

She squeezed that section of her face just above the top of her nose and the eyelids between her eyebrows. I've only ever seen her do that when she was in the dean's office with me or when she'd just come home from a long shift at the hospital, so I knew that this wasn't good. It wasn't good at all.

"Kadeem!" she shouted like she'd just thought about something. "Who you been staying with? What you been eating?"

"I'm fine, Ma," I said.

"Fine?"

"I am." I really was. I wanted to say "*oh, now you wanna know*," but I didn't cause I really was fine. Why be rude by sounding rude? I was actually doing okay, more than okay, really. I knew exactly what to do and how to do it. I knew how to wash my uniforms and hang them just right so that I wouldn't have to iron them before wearing them to school. I walked to school every day with Tess like nothing changed. The only real difference was that Grandad wasn't there to walk us home. That was a lonely thing that colored our walks home. That old saying, "you don't miss something till it's gone?" It was true with Grandad. I missed him like I missed air conditioning in my bedroom. Although Tess knew how to break off the sugar cane without cutting her hands, it still didn't feel the same watching her. I actually missed Grandad breaking off the sugar cane and passing it my way, the sugar cane that belonged to our *people*.

In one of my visits to the hospital, Grandad told me where to find cash to use for my lunch. He had it well hidden too. Not that I was looking, but if I was, I would've never found it. I found it in the place he told me and used just what I needed, nothing more. Plus, now I had lots of help. I ate dinner with Tess' family each night Grandad was in the hospital. The neighbors, even the neighbor that Grandad *didn't* steal the golden apples from, brought over food for me to eat. I didn't even know how they knew Grandad was in the hospital, but they acted like I knew who they were and they knew me. It was weird at first accepting help, but they wouldn't let me say no. Each day after school, Tess' dad took me to see Grandad. He'd say a quick hi to Grandad and then disappear for about an hour. That gave me and Grandad plenty of time to talk even more than we had during dinner time. The doctors didn't tell me what was wrong. They kept insisting that they couldn't cause I was a child, but Grandad did. Grandad talked with me like he knew I'd understand what was happening. He talked with me like he trusted that I'd be okay, no matter what. He said he had a mild stroke. Even though he laughed when he said it, I didn't find it funny at all. But he was laughing again, so that was good. He even laughed when I told him about the washing machine that I found in his little house out back that was in perfect working order. I didn't find that funny either cause he had me washing my uniform by hand each night after the beach. But he laughed, laughed so hard that he started coughing. Each night I'd visit, he'd tell me he was coming home soon, and that's what I told Ma, that even though he had a stroke, a mild one, he was coming home soon and she didn't have to worry.

"I'll be there soon," Ma said.

"Ma, we'll be fine. Grandad will be out soon and everything will be back to normal." I said it like I believed it cause really, I did. Things were gonna be back to normal, a new normal any way - a better normal.

DINNERS WITH TESS' family were not as strange as they'd been the first few nights. One, eating dinner with my girlfriend's family, especially with her father, was not on the top of my bucket list. Two, eating dinner with the school's principal, headmaster, whatever he was called, would NEVER ever be on my bucket list.

When I got the invite, I didn't think there was an option for me to say no. One, I'd probably be offending Tess' by saying no and I definitely didn't want to upset the very first person who was nice to me for no reason. And, two, I would be offending Tess for saying no to her dad, the headmaster. Saying No wasn't going to be good for me no matter how I said it. So, I said *yes* and *thank you* like the good young man I was becoming.

The first night was the strangest. This was the night that I met Tess' mother. She looked like an older version of Tess. Her hair was natural too, face round, and eyes just as big and bright as Tess'. She was friendly too, asking a lot of questions, especially for someone who I'd just met.

She and I were in the kitchen when she asked, "How you liking it down here in dis hot way'da?"

"It's ok," I said.

"Ok?" she laughed, "nuttin okay bout dis way'da. E so hot dat mosquito a bruk off day wing dem and a use dem to fan day-self."

"Yes, it's hot," I agreed, "but it's not as hot as where we live." Grandad lived on a hill; we felt all the breeze from the ocean up there. The only real heat was when we were in the house and the doors weren't opened. The breeze was good, my body was also getting used to the weather here. Clothes weren't sticking to me the way they used to when I first got here. My shirts blew in the wind just like everyone else's.

"So, how you like de school?" she asked, "it much different from 'merica? Bet you ain't expec' to like it like you do. Tess, say you like it. She say you really like de band."

"It's ok. School isn't really that different," I lied, "naw, I mean, no ma'am, I didn't really expect to like it the way I do."

"Yeah, Mommy, you goin' hear him when we play for Carnival." Tess walked in the kitchen; her dad followed.

Their kitchen was much bigger than Grandad's. Unlike Grandad's combined living room, dining room, and kitchen separated by pieces of furniture, this kitchen was like a real kitchen: stove and sink and lots of kitchen stuff just in the kitchen. They also didn't have a microwave. Four round vibrantly colored table mats neatly surrounded a short vase of red hibiscuses on a round table. Mrs. Headmaster started plating the food and handing it to Tess. The scent of freshly cooked food filled the air. It was definitely a different scent, different from the burnt oil aroma that filled your nostrils from a Popeye's chicken box. Why didn't Ma cook more?

"Sit here," Tess guided me to one of the chairs. Even though it was a round table, I still didn't want to just sit anywhere without permission. I could hear Grandad saying *doan sit anywhere at a man's table, le' him tell you way to sit,* or something like that but with a round table, there was no real place I could sit to do any of those things. Tess made it easy by pointing out where to sit.

"Thank you!" I said. She put one of the plates in front of me after serving her dad. She and her mom were the last to sit. An entire fish, eyes, tail, sat on my plate with black eyed peas and rice, fried plantains and this thing that Grandad called dasheen - not my favorite cause it tasted like chalky white potato. I immediately started eating. I hadn't even noticed how hungry I'd been at the hospital, but the truth was that I hadn't even eaten at lunch nor had I at breakfast. In fact, I hadn't had breakfast since Grandad was in the hospital. All the food that the neighbors brought over still didn't fix the fact that Grandad wasn't there, so I didn't eat breakfast, and now I was trying to fill that hole in my belly.

"A-hem," Tess actually said, *Ahem* instead of clearing her throat. All eyes were glued on me, including the fish.

"I know you grand-far-da does bless he food before he eat it," Tess' dad said.

"Yes," I lied. I should've told him that Grandad said dead things didn't need blessing; it's the live ones that do but instead I swallowed the food I'd already put in my mouth, lowered my head, closed my eyes, and waited for Tess' father to bless the dead food on our plates.

CHAPTER 18

With each visit, Grandad was getting better and better, stronger even. They even moved him out of the room with the other beds and patients and into his own private room where he could move around without disturbing anyone. This room had a window that looked out and across to the other wing of the hospital. Not an amazing view. Large concrete pots, filled with only dirt, lined the walk way. No flowers. No trees. No beach, but we could still see when visitors, doctors, and nurses passed. That was better for us because it allowed Grandad to talk and laugh as loudly as he wanted. He laughed so loudly sometimes that we'd hear doors slam occasionally. Door slamming only made us laugh harder because Grandad would say, "is wa happen to dem day eh, day never hear people happy befor'?" Grandad was even moving around on his own; slowly, but still on his own. He'd drag himself around the bed, pressing his palm on every part of the bed until he got where he wanted to go. He refused to let anyone help him. He would even swat the nurses' hands away when they tried to keep him from falling. "Me got han' an' foot before you, eh," he would say to them, "and me know how to use dem."

It didn't seem at all that the nurses were enjoying Grandad's stay in the hospital, at least when I visited. Although they smiled at me, the smile disappeared as soon as Grandad looked away. He reminded me of my own expression to avoid trouble: fake a smile just for the sake of it. One day a nurse was making his bed when he was in the bathroom, and as soon as he came out and saw what she was doing, he immediately started to complain.

"Is wa you mek-in up de bed fa, a goin' right back in day." He moved as fast as he could, slower than his usual "Grandad-speed," just so that he could get back into the bed and the nurse could not finish.

"Grandad, don't be difficult," I said.

"Difficult? Is wok she givin' she self," Grandad rolled his eyes at her. "Lemme tell you sum-ting, Kadeem." He looked straight at me after getting back into the unmade bed, "Doan go mek no ness-a-ssary wok fuh you-self. It mek sense she mek up de bed like me naw go back in day just dis minute?"

"No, Grandad, it doesn't," I agreed.

"Den wa she doin' it for? Strupes."

"So, next time Ma complains about me making the bed, I'm going to say that Grandad says it doesn't make sense." I laughed.

"Bwoy," he laughed, "doan go tell you mud-da I tell you to disobey she eh. You still gah to do what she say. If she tell you slice a slice bread," he breathed heavily for a moment, "slice it!"

Stubbornly, he also refused to take any medicine. On one of my visits, I overheard the doctor tell him that he had to start taking his medicine. Tess' dad had just walked out when the doctor entered and immediately started on Grandad.

"You won't even let the nurse put in your IV," the doctor said to Grandad. I guessed he was tired of asking me to leave with Grandad telling him I could stay. The doc looked as though he had just graduated from doctor school, maybe even high school. His white coat wasn't ironed, something that I knew for a fact Grandad noticed, and his shoes were not clean, something that Ma would definitely notice. His beard barely grew in all the places that it was supposed to. Patches dotted his face. In fact, he looked tired, like he'd been up all night, not doctoring.

"Da poison ar' you tryin' to put in me body no no good fe me," Grandad said, shaking his head.

"Sir, this medicine has been tested and proven. Never has a stroke patient gotten worse from the administering of this medicine. You really have to think about your health!"

"Is tink-ing a tink-ing a know me no want dat in me body, tall," he replied.

The full IV bag stayed on the skinny silver pole in the corner of the room hidden away like an unwanted step child.

"Tomorrow I'm going to bring you some literature on this medicine, so you will be able to see the research behind its effectiveness."

"Bring all de lit-tra-tra you want, I gon' drink me bush tea and every-ting gon' be aw-right, watch wa I say," Grandad said forcefully.

There was no way he was going to take that medicine. Once he said it, that was the end of that. He reminded me of the time that Ma wanted me to try fried okras. She swore up and down that I would love them if I only gave them a chance. She even offered to buy a Nintendo Switch if I just ate one fried okra. I wanted the Nintendo Switch. She knew I wanted it too, so it was good bait if I tried her stupid fried okra. I didn't try it, and I didn't get that Nintendo switch. The doctor wrinkled his nose, squeezed his eyes shut, and twisted his mouth like Ma did when she was tired of trying everything.

"When are you coming home," I asked one day as he slowly moved around his bed.

"Soon come," he said.

"Okay," I said, trying to believe it.

He had said it, and frankly, he looked better. He was starting to stand up a little more often and with more strength than in previous days, still with a curve in his back, but stronger. While my time with him wasn't the same as when we had walked from school or on the beach or even as I watched him play his type of football, it was still a treat to sit with Grandad and listen to his stories. Although I thought that most of his stories were made up just to distract me from whatever game we were playing, I still enjoyed them. For instance, one time as we played dominoes, he told me a story about seeing a jack-a-lantern on the bridge.

"One time when I was bout young like you," his hands shook as he shuffled the dominoes, "we was walking home from de beach, not de one we does go to, mat-ta-a-fak dis is why me doan go dung da side no mo," he reminisced.

"You were young like me?" I laughed.

"Wa you tink, I born ol' like dis, strupes," he shook his head, "de great Bob Marley used to say dat gray hair is a crown a glory eh."

"Bob Marley didn't say that, Grandad," I laughed again.

He handed me my share of the dominoes, and of course then drew the highest number, so he played first.

"Is who say so den, since you know every-ting?"

"It's in the Bible, Grandad." I had to draw another domino because none in my hand matched the board, and now I had even more dominoes to get rid of.

"Strupes," Grandad sucked his teeth, "how you know dat and me never see you read de Bible one time since you ya?"

"Ma used to read it to me all the time, and then we started memorizing scriptures when I was older, so I know for a certifiable fact that's not from Bob Marley, unless Bob Marley is some unknown book of the Bible I ain't never hear about."

"Well, you wrong pon dis one." He matched a domino to the board. His dominoes disappeared as I collected more and more. Not the way to win the game, at least for me. Matter of fact, I don't think I'd ever won a game of anything with Grandad.

"Ok, okay, you're right," I surrendered, "tell me this story."

"So, me and me friend dem was walking back from de beach, E wasn't to late but de sun had dung gone dung. We was walking under de bridge, de one way de locomotive use to carry de sugar cane from de field to de factory," he began.

"Yeah," I nodded like I understood. I was really trying to concentrate on my hand of dominoes.

"En-e-way, e was bout tree a we." He looked down at his hand. "We was eating sea grapes. You get any sea grapes since you come?"

"No, Grandad, you said they weren't in season yet," I reminded him.

"Okay, you got to get some, day sweet, man. Deese ones we was eating da day was de sweetest I ever had." He closed his eyes and faked licked his fingers. "Me no even tink I ever had sea grapes so sweet after dat."

"Oh, ok," I said, hoping that he'd finish up the story quickly so that I could get a new hand of dominoes. I clearly wasn't going to win this one, yet again.

"So, a tell you e wasn't dark dark, but e was dark enough to see dis bright bright fire shape lak a man comin' to-wards us. All a we wipe we eye dem lak' we no see wa we see. E was lak' a man shaped lak' de sun was walking towards we, flames all roun' he. Of course, me a tink dat de sun cyan walk, so me naw see wa me see."

"You're making this up, Grandad!"

"Mek wa up? Bwoy, a wish me no see wa me see." He added another domino. "De ting was walking fass, so til an' all a we foot dem was lak' day in a cement, none a we move," he continued.

"You just stood there and watched it come towards you?"

"Wa we was gon do?"

"Run," I suggested, "this is a man on fire, right?"

"A man pon fy-ya?" Grandad steadily added dominoes to the board. "Is a man pon fy-ya you say? If we had see a man pon fy-ya, we would-a just help he out, chow some water pon him or some-ting. No, dis more dan a man pon fy-ya; dis ya was a jack-a-lan-ton."

"So, what did you do? Did you make it out of there alive?" I realized my stupid question after it left my mouth.

"Is me tellin' you de story bout me, you know? Wa mumu question dat *if we mek it out alive*?" Grandad laughed.

I laughed too, but I wanted to hear more about this jack-o-lantern. All I knew about jack-o-lanterns was that they were pumpkins people carved out during Halloween to put a light in. The light would glow through the carved-out areas making the pumpkin's face of eyes, nose, and mouth glow. However, this was some next level stuff Grandad was talking. His jack-o-lantern had legs and moved on its own.

"Non a we foot dem move, and de ting was getting nearer and nearer, so close dat we could hear de hair pon we head frying and falling to de grung." He looked up at me continuing, "you see how dem slice pig sound when a fry dem fuh you?"

"Bacon, Grandad?"

"Yeah, dem," he said as he continued to add dominoes to the board. "Das wa we hair had sound lak' when dis ting get closer. Kadeem, ask me how close dis ting was."

"How close, Grandad?"

"Bwoy, de ting was so close dat e bun off all we clothes stand-in' right day in de floor dat had tun into cement. All a we was standin' day ne'kid as we bawn," he said.

"Oh my God, Grandad,"

"E like e was so hot 'gainst we body dat e bun we foot dem free. As soon as dat happen, we tek off wid a runnin', me no know who was behin' me, but all me no was me wasn't de las' one, so me wasn't gon' be de fus' one dis ting catch." Bam! Grandad shook the table when he slammed his last domino down. "Is win a win again eh," he trumpeted proudly.

"You cheated, Grandad," I pointed out.

"How I cheat?"

"You didn't give me a chance to play my hand," I complained.

"Is me tell you doan play? Wa you tink we was doin' here all dis time? Playin' dominoes, strupes," he said.

"Yeah, but...,"

"Yeah, but nuttin', wa you learn from dis story?"

"That you a cheater," I complained.

"Uh un, you naw pay attention, Kadeem." He squinted his eyes and wagged his index finger at me, "once you out in front, doan look back, ain't nut-ting back day but some jack-a-lan-tun' tryin' to bun you up."

Just as I was about to ask Grandad what he was talking about, there was a knock on the door.

"Is who dat?" Grandad looked up.

"It's me, daddy." Ma opened the door slowly and walked in. She wasn't wearing her scrubs or her ugly nonslip shoes, but an actual dress. Her hair, usually in a ponytail, was curled to hang down the middle of her back. Painfully, she looked like time away from me had done her some good. Well, I was fine too. In fact, time away from her had done me some good too!

"Ma!" I yelled and jumped up to hug her. She let go of her rolling bag so that she could wrap both arms around me. I wrapped both my arms around her too. I hadn't realized how much I'd missed her, till then.

"Gwendolyn, is wa you come dung here fa? Strupes," Grandad said as he started to drag himself from the table to the bed.

"Daddy, lemme help you." Ma lightly moved me aside to help Grandad.

"Gyal, you tink me is one a you pay-shunt dem? Me no need no help," he said.

"Stop it, daddy." Ma tried to help him on to the bed. Grandad swatted her arms just as he did the nurses who worked here. But, unlike the nurses here, Ma didn't let up. "The doctor says that you haven't been taking your medicine," she said.

"You mean de likkle bwoy out day wid he dutty shoes and rumple up dack-ta jacket talk 'bout he a dack-ta?"

"Daddy, please," Ma pleaded with him, "please just do what they say."

"Do wa day say?" Grandad coughed. "You tink me gon.." He coughed. "Lay some...," he coughed again.

"Daddy, drink some water." Ma held the glass of water to his mouth trying to feed it to him, but he pushed it away.

By now, Grandad coughed uncontrollably. Ma tried to sit him upright patting him on his back as one trying to burp a baby.

Coughing didn't stop. Grandad seemed to have lost control of his neck so his head fell back.

"Daddy," Ma yelled, "Kadeem go get de doctor!"

Ma's accent rang deep.

I stood there, legs unmoving, looking at what was going on like I was watching a tv show, but this was happening right in front of me. Grandad and Ma were the actors, while I was only the viewer, waiting and watching to see what was going to happen next.

"Kadeem," Ma yelled, "go, now!"

I took off running just as if a jack-o-lantern chased me. The dirty-shoes-wearing doctor was at the end of the hallway talking to a nurse.

"Grandad," I breathed heavily, "something's wrong."

The doctor ran past me towards Grandad's room. I ran, following him back to Grandad's room, like I was about to do some doctoring too. Ma wiped something from Grandad's mouth but still held him upright when we rushed in.

"He started foaming at the mouth; he hasn't responded to anything I've tried," Ma said clearly.

The doctor nodded his head, said something into the remote on the bed and then started to work on Grandad himself. Several nurses ran in after the doctor's call.

"We've got to get a line in," The doctor said to one of the nurses. She ran around to the side of the bed and tapped Grandad's arm.

"Common', Kadeem," Ma said.

"No, I wanna stay with Grandad."

"We have to let them do their jobs."

"Ma, please, I can't," I pleaded, "I can't leave him."

"You can't stay here."

"But, I have to," I protested, "I have to!"

CHAPTER 19

B oth of us sat in the small waiting room yearning for someone, anyone, to tell us something. The seats, similar to those at the airport, felt cold; metal and though singular, they were still joined together so there was a handle between me and Ma. A large fan hung from the ceiling spinning so fast that it shook, an annoying sound from the metal hanging string knocking against its blades.

"This is a hospital for Christ's sake," she said, looking up at the spinning blades, "shouldn't it be quieter than this?"

"I don't know, Ma," I replied.

"I don't understand it," Ma shook her head. "So, you just found him like that?"

"Yeah."

"You didn't see any signs?"

"Naw," I shook my head, "nothing."

"It still doesn't make any sense."

"I mean, Ma," I said, "I know he's old, but he don't even really act like an old man."

"I know."

"He's always playing soccer."

"Football," Ma corrected me.

"He could out-swim a shark."

"That's true," Ma laughed.

"He don't even eat bad."

"He's always been like that."

"You know, when I finally realized that there was a KFC here, I begged him to take me, but he wouldn't!" I laughed. "I don't even like KFC."

"Yeah, he's not going to do that," Ma shook her head.

"I figured he wouldn't after he said, *me naw go pay-* "

"Nobody to hot no pot fa me," Ma finished, and we both laughed. "I don't even think we've ever eaten out."

"I could believe that," I said, "we've been eating nothing but what he cooks since I've been here."

"Actually, there was this one time," Ma smiled, "when I was little, Daddy took me to this place. He said we were going to eat pizza. I remember how excited I was because I always wanted to try this thing that Lisa and her friends on *Saved by the Bell* used to eat after school."

"*Saved by the Bell*?" I asked.

"*90201*?"

"Nope," I shook my head, "Ma, I'm like a hundred years younger than you."

"Boy, stop."

"Are those shows even on tv anymore?"

"Probably not. I ain't never heard of them,"

"You guys don't have shows about kids in high school anymore," she covered her face with her hand, "this generation is missing out, man."

"Yeah, Ma, we got shows about high school. We got *Liv & Maddie*."

"What?"

"*Invincible* is the best actually. These are a bunch of high school kids," I said, "but it's superheroes so I doubt they eat pizza."

"Strupes," Ma sucked her teeth, "I'm talking about real shows about real life, not that made up stuff. Anyway, Daddy said he was taking me to get pizza. I was so excited, right."

"Excited about pizza?"

"Yes, of course!" she said a little too high. "You don't get it; this man never ever took me to eat out anywhere! Always gotta catch the food or grow it."

Oh, but now I did get it. Not only did we pass by a KFC on the way to the market every Saturday, but we passed a Domino's Pizza, Burger King, and a Subway on the island too. Places that I love, except KFC. I'll only eat that if there's no Popeye's. Not once did Grandad ever offer to take me to any of these places. Unlike Ma, who was always ordering in or eating out, Grandad didn't. He literally caught his food and cooked it.

"I get it, now," I said.

"Back then, he had a VW Bug, so we crammed into his car and rode into town." She smiled again at a good memory. "Let me tell you how excited I was. We were actually going into town to eat out, but not just eat out, but eat pizza."

"Ok, Ma, it's pizza, I get it," I laughed.

"So, we drove all the way into town, past the roundabout, not the one by the airport because that wasn't there at the time."

"It wasn't?"

"No, that's fairly new, anyway," she continued, "Daddy parked the car in front of a thatched roof bamboo hut draped in ice, green and gold flags."

"Ice, green, and gold?"

"Rasta colors: red, green, and yellow."

"Oh, ok."

"Yeah, so I'm thinking there's no way this thing could stand up during a hurricane, right?"

"Right," I agreed.

"Anyway, we're in this shack, and I'm thinking that Lisa probably wouldn't like this, right?"

"Lisa?"

"Yeah, Lisa," she rolled her eyes at me, "from *Saved by the Bell*! You're not listening, Kadeem?"

"Yeah, Ma."

"Anyway, there's this tall Rasta man selling pizza. The menu was written on a piece of board and tacked on to one of the bamboo poles that was holding up the thatched roof. I remember Daddy telling me I could order whatever I wanted."

"That's good, right?"

"Yeah, that's good," Ma laughed, "but what I wanted wasn't on the menu. Yeah, it was pizza. Yeah, I always wanted pizza, but all the toppings were ve-ja-tables!" It didn't matter what accent Ma used, words like vegetable and comfortable always sounded like there was an actual table at the end.

"You love you a salad, Ma, so you could've ordered that veggie pizza," I suggested.

"No, Kadeem," she laughed again, "I'm talking ve-ja-tables like dasheen, carrots, peas... "

"Peas?" I laughed, "on a pizza?"

"Yeah, peas... on a pizza." Ma shook her head, "it was as though he just put everything he had on the top of some dough and called it a pizza, it was so nasty Kadeem," she said.

"That's why you don't like pizza now!" I laughed so hard that I had to hold my stomach.

"Yeah, no pizza for me," Ma laughed too, "we better be quiet in the people's hospital!"

"Yeah," I sighed remembering where we were and why we were there.

"Well, it looks good on you, Kadeem!" Ma looked me up and down. "This place, you look like you're happy!"

"I didn't look good before?" I asked, "I didn't look happy?" I knew what she meant. You could actually see an improvement of muscles in my shoulders and in my legs even hidden behind my uniform. Without my uniform, a budding six pack was slowly emerging on my stomach. It must've been all the swimming I was doing. Either way, Ma was right. I looked good. I felt good too, finally happy.

"Ah-hem," Tess cleared her throat. She and her dad stood in the waiting area looking at us. I hadn't even realized but the sun broke through the window, met us.

I jumped up, "Ma, this is Tess and..."

"Lenwell," Ma said before I could finish.

"Gwen," the headmaster breathed as he moved past me, paused, looked at Ma as though he was asking permission, and then moved in to hug her. They both awkwardly tried to figure out which arm to put around each other; then they just stood still and hugged for a crazy long time, like I was watching them in slow motion.

"How have you been?" Ma released the hold first.

"I've been well," the headmaster brushed an imaginary speck off his tie. "You, how are you?"

"Doing okay," Ma answered, "umm, thanks for feeding Kadeem. He's been telling me how he's been at your house every night for dinner. I appreciate that."

"No problem," he said.

"And thanks for bringing him in here daily to see Daddy."

"No problem at all," the headmaster said.

A really long silence broke before Tess said, "Aw you eat?"

"Naw," I admitted. I was really hungry too as I hadn't eaten since lunch the previous day. I felt a major hole in my stomach by now.

"A bring you some-ting." Tess handed me a small brown paper bag with oil spots all over it. I hoped that it was beef patties cause that'd fill that empty spot right about now. "A didn't know you mud-da was here dough so..."

"It's okay," Ma said, "I'm not really that hungry anyway."

"Sorry," Tess apologized.

"So," I said to Ma, "this is Tess,"

"I figured, Kadeem," Ma said, "she's just as pretty as you said she was."

"Maaaa," I complained.

"Hello, Tess." Ma smiled at Tess, "you've been keeping my son out of trouble I hear."

"Trouble. He is de trouble," Tess declared.

"Oh, is that so?" Ma's eyes widened.

"Yeah, he funny too; he does keep me laughing lak' he a comedian or some-ting." Tess moved closer to me and slipped her hand in mine. Ma's eyes dropped directly on the action as though this scene also played in slow motion.

"Kadeem's funny?" Ma said, as if she doubted my comedic skills for real. "Okay, Kadeem, tell us a joke."

"Stop it Ma." I shook my head. Did she really expect me to tell a joke on the spot like this?

"He's funny," Tess confirmed. "He does make me laugh all de time."

"See?" I said, assuredly, "happy customer."

Tess squeezed my hand. She hid a piece of her lower lip in her mouth, biting on it the way she did when the English teacher went ham on her. She couldn't have been nervous to meet Ma. Could she? I gave her hand a quick squeeze to let her know she was doing great. I hoped she received my signal and relaxed.

There was a short silence before Tess asked, "You hear anything yet?" Just then, the doctor walked into the waiting room, his white coat still ruffled and shoes still dirty.

"I will need to speak to the immediate family." He said in a tone of someone who had bad news. He didn't look like one of those doctors who came to tell the family that they were able to save the leg they thought they were going to lose. Instead, he looked like he was about to tell us something that we should probably be sitting to hear.

"It's all right," Ma said, "everyone here is family."

"Your father suffered a myocardial infarction," Doctor Dirty Shoes said softly.

"A what?" I asked.

"A heart attack," Ma explained.

"Grandad had a heart attack?" There was no way this man who moved about like he was my age had a heart attack. I wasn't no doctor but I wasn't gonna believe that. No way.

"We caught it in time," Doctor Dirty Shoes continued. "Obviously, if he had been taking the medicine," he paused, "we probably wouldn't be at this point…"

"We don't know that," Ma interjected.

"Actually," Doc sounded as if he was about to argue with Ma but changed his mind. "Nevertheless, we were able to perform a carotid endarterectomy to unblock his clogged artery." He said this stuff like my Grandad was some big old man who didn't swim every day, didn't play soccer every day, didn't take care of himself! Grandad was not a "clogged artery" person, not at all.

"Is he going to be okay?" I asked.

"He'll be fine," the doc assured us, "we'll keep him under observation for a couple of days and he'll be back in your hands shortly."

"Thank you," Ma shook his hand.

"Can I see him now?" I asked.

"He won't be up for visitors for some time," the doctor said. "Tomorrow will probably be best."

"Thank you," Ma said to the doctor.

"I can take you home, Gwen," the headmaster suggested.

"That won't be necessary," Ma refused, like she had a car or something. "You've done enough for us already and I appreciate that."

"It's no trouble, you know, Gwen," the headmaster pressed, "I was going to take the children home anyway; I just didn't know you were here."

"And miss school?" I asked.

"Yes," the headmaster answered, "it's been a long day, and the day hasn't even really started yet. I'll let your teachers know what is happening."

"Thank you," I said. He was right. It had already been a long day. I felt like if I sat anywhere, I'd fall asleep. I slept the night before, but only a little, not enough to stay fully awake in all my classes, certainly not in that English woman's class. I was certainly grateful for the time off, but still worried about Grandad.

We all rode silently in the headmaster's small van. Ma stared out the window as the sugar cane fields whisked by, just like when we first got here, when she first dropped me off. However, in the dead of night, like we were running from something. She didn't know the taxi driver like she seemed to know *Lewell*. My thoughts were different now though. I didn't get into things that didn't concern me anymore. Like Grandad said, it didn't make me a man. Plus, what trouble could I get into? Did this school have a dean? Come to think about it, I didn't remember seeing anyone walking around patrolling the verandah like they patrolled the hallways in Orlando. Once in a while, the headmaster strolled by, but I guess that was normal since his daughter was in my class. Other than that, everything here was "*irie*" like Grandad said it would be. I was a different person here. I really like it here and hoped that Grandad in the hospital wouldn't change things. My life was gonna be different; I could feel it already. How? I wasn't sure, but I also wasn't about to let Ma take me back. Not now.

CHAPTER 20

Ma was getting on my nerves, literally. It was as if she had nothing to do but to get under my skin. I was glad she was here - kinda glad, anyway. But, Grandad and I had already built a great routine, and here she came, messing things up. She walked around the house in the dead of night when I needed my sleep, and slammed drawers and utensils. To make things worse, after a clatter she'd tiptoe into my room and say *did I wake you*? Umh, any noise that loud would wake a bear in hibernation. One night she rearranged the kitchen so the clanging of the pots and pans woke me up just as I drifted asleep. What was she doing? This was going to definitely make Grandad mad cause he liked things where he liked them. But then again, I'd never seen him mad at anything for any reason. Even when drivers would cut him off to the point of nearly crashing, he still had no reaction. I, on the other hand, would probably have some choice words to spit at the driver who couldn't hear me anyway.

I guessed that she couldn't sleep, but that didn't mean that I didn't want to sleep either. Another night she moved furniture in the living room. Chairs dragged across the tiled floor like they didn't want to be moved, but Ma just forced them. One day after school the plant from the tv disappeared and the tv was no longer against its original wall but up against a window. That made no sense to me, putting it against the window like that, but I guessed that it did make the room bigger. Surprisingly, that worked although it looked like it didn't. Or, maybe I thought it didn't work because Grandad never turned it on. Either way, it was fully equipped with an Apple TV and lots of streaming channels. Why didn't Grandad use it? Nevertheless, Ma was changing everything. I really wished that she'd go home, but I knew that wasn't going to happen with Grandad still in the hospital.

She tried to make me breakfast before school too, something she wouldn't normally do. Unlike Grandad, she burnt everything, even the plantains. Who burnt plantains? They were the easiest things to fry - a little oil, watch them brown, then flip them, then remove them from the frying pan.

"Ma?" I asked one day, "why don't you know how to cook?"

"I do," she replied, "I know how to cook."

"How come you always burn everything? Grandad don't do that."

"No, he doesn't," she sat for a moment as though she was defeated. "He's been cooking for me since I could remember to be honest. Breakfast would be ready by the time I woke up and dinner would be ready by the time I got home from school."

"Sounds like a great parent," I laughed. Ma didn't do any of that stuff me. I always had cereal and milk though and plenty of take-out menus in the kitchen. I wasn't starving but I didn't realize that I was missing homemade food until Grandad.

"He was," her eyes welled up. "He is. He's a great parent."

"Yeah," I agreed.

"Daddy tried, though," she reminisced. "We'd go to the beach sometimes and we'd dive for our dinner –"

"We do that," I said, proudly.

"We'd catch all sorts of different fish and he'd call out the name of each one like they were old relatives. We even caught a squid once."

"Did you eat it?"

"No, I can't eat nothing that look like it should be in a horror movie."

I laughed, "we've never caught a squid."

"We'd come home with the food, set up the coal pot."

"Why doesn't he use the stove? Doesn't it work?"

"Yeah, it works, but it's a whole process. You gotta light the gas oven. It's not like ours where you just turn a nob and it's on. Plus, daddy always says it's better to cook in the open air with natural lights." She smiled.

"Oh," I said. "He's never used it since I've been here.

"Any way," she continued, "once Daddy set up the coal pot, I'd disappear."

"Disappear?" I asked, "where would you go?"

"I'd go in my room or go "do homework,"" she curled her fingers and imitated air quotes as she said *do homework*.

"Ma, you lied?" I said playfully.

"Not really," she admitted. "I really just didn't like cooking, plus he did it so well without me that I didn't think being out there was helping."

"Man, Ma, we could've been eating good food this entire time," I joked. "Did you guys stop going to the beach after Grandad realized you just wanted the food but didn't want to work for it? Cause I don't think he'd let me do that."

She laughed, "not even. We still went to the beach but we spent most of the time sitting on the sand and watching the ocean move. Those were peaceful days."

"Yeah, I like those days too," I mused. "No matter how far we looked, the sea just never seemed to end."

"Yeah," Ma sighed. "But it's one of the most peaceful moments you'll ever have in life."

I nodded my head in agreement. Even when it was just me and Tess, we'd sit on the sand, backs to the land and toes buried with the water washing ashore only to clean the sand from our toes just to be buried again. I could sit there all day.

"I wish we had that in Orlando."

"Me too," Ma agreed. "You know, no matter how far we look, we could never see the end of the ocean?"

"Okay?" I questioned. "You alright, Ma?"

"Yeah," she seemed to have snapped herself out of the memory she was having. "I'm good.

Ma continued to cook or what she considered to be cooking. The scent reminded me of why she didn't cook in Orlando. Each morning the house smelt like burnt something because Ma didn't even bother to open any windows when she cooked. This may be the reason that Grandad cooked almost everything on the coal pot outside, because of the smell in the house - something I didn't think Ma knew how to do. Plus, Grandad didn't burn food. I'd bring home lobsters, crabs, wilks, whatever I caught for dinner, but as in Orlando, by the time I got home, in true Ma-fashion, a half-eaten box of KFC on the table waited for me because she'd already burnt our food where we couldn't eat it. I guessed I should be grateful that she was trying, but I knew Grandad would say *know wa you good at an' do dat*. Ma was not good at cooking. She needed to stop trying. Eventually, I just stopped: stopped bringing home food that I caught. But I'd not stopped going to the beach. Beaching would never end as long as I had any control over it.

"You out here washing clothes?" Ma asked me one day.

"Yeah, they dirty." I was hand washing my uniform after coming from the beach, something that I was used to at this point.

"You know, you could just use the washer that's in the little house, right?"

"Yeah, I know." I continued washing the clothes and later hung them on the clothesline, "but it's just my uniform, not enough for the washer."

"Really," Ma laughed, "is this the same kid who would ask me to wash one shirt just to match an outfit?"

"Same kid," I replied.

"Lawd, Jesus, is what happen to you?" her accent came out deep on that one.

"Nothing, Ma," I hung the clothes, "same old Kadeem."

"Naw, this is Kadeem 2.0," she smiled. "Is that what they say? An upgrade. I like it, I like it a lot!"

Although Tess and I were still able to go to the beach after school and hang out as Grandad healed, Lenwell, Mr. Headmaster still took us to the hospital some evenings. He'd pick up Ma before school ended and we'd go together. The rides were always silent and awkward. Ma would ride in front and me and Tess would ride in the back while Ma looked out the window, me and Tess just looked at each other wondering why no one spoke. Normally, me and Tess did not talk while we were with her dad, but this was weird. Two grown-ups, who obviously knew each other, said nothing but *good afternoon* and *thanks a lot*. Either way, I was sure that Ma was glad for the ride. If not for Lenwell, we'd be taking the bus which, as they whizzed by, did not look safe at all. Passengers or not, even if Grandad was about to turn a corner, they'd still pass us. Crazy!

Both of Grandad's vehicles stood in the yard, untouched and unmoved, since the night I drove him to the hospital. "Why don't you just drive Grandad's car, Ma?" I suggested one day.

"I don't like to drive here."

"But it'll be so much easier." I didn't mind riding with Tess' dad, but it was obvious how awkward it was whether she wanted to admit it or not. I mean, she was quiet during every ride. "I'm sure Grandad wouldn't mind," I added.

"I really don't like driving here," she admitted, "the roads are narrow, people don't have patience, plus everything is on the wrong side of the road."

"Yeah, but it's not so bad. Grandad lets me drive all the time," I confessed.

"What?!" Ma seemed surprised.

"Yeah, he doesn't even drive anymore," I lied. "I'm like his personal driver."

"Strupes," Ma sucked her teeth, "now I know you're lying cause Daddy don't ever let people drive his cars!"

"He let me," I said confidently.

"Ok, if you say so, Kadeem," she said doubtfully.

"Well, I did," I laughed. "You know, I run these streets, right?"

"Right," she grimaced.

"I took him to the hospital," I went on.

"You didn't call the ambulance, Kadeem?"

"No, Grandad didn't want me to."

"That does sound like him," Ma admitted.

"Yeah," I agreed.

THE DAY FINALLY CAME when Grandad was released from the hospital. "Released" sounded like he was in jail or something, but for Grandad, being kept in that hospital was exactly like being in jail. I knew he was coming home too, so school seemed a little longer that day. It was like Christmas when I knew that Ma was getting me what I really wanted, but I had to wait until 12:01 a.m. to open my present, usually a video game I'd been scoping out. Grandad coming home felt like it was about to be Christmas Day, 12:01 a.m.

"You excited, Kadeem?" Tess asked.

"Yeah." I was actually. I totally missed being around him even though he cheated at games and stole the *people's* sugar cane on walks home from school, along with the golden apples that belonged to his neighbor which hung in his yard. Grandad had a strange way of explaining things but, when I really sat down and thought about it, he was mostly right.

We skipped the beach that day so that we could go straight home. Tess and I walked from the school directly to my house just in time to see Tess' dad's minivan drive up the hill. He parked outside the fence instead of going inside with Grandad; however, Ma opened the bigger gate.

"See dem day," Tess said.

"Yeah," we quickened our steps, almost running to get to the top of the hill.

"Bwoy," Grandad said, "school done a-ready?"

"A long time ago," I said, "lemme help you Grandad,"

"A got it," he fanned me away. "A got it, all are you ack-ting lak'a dead a some-ting."

"Well..." I said.

"Daddy, you're going to have to let us help you," Ma demanded, "the doctor said..."

"De dack-ta say wa? Strupes," Grandad sucked his teeth.

He still couldn't stand up entirely on his own, so although he refused our help, he still relied on both Ma and the headmaster to walk inside. Ma and the headmaster shifted sideways with Grandad's arms draped over them so that they could all fit through the smaller gate. That I didn't understand because Ma had already opened the wider gate probably to avoid this very thing. They both helped Grandad lift each leg on the steps to help him inside. I imagined that the headmaster could just lift Grandad and take him inside, but he didn't. Grandad would probably fight him off first before that ever happened.

"Is wa dis?" Grandad asked as he entered the house. I knew he wouldn't like it. "Are you done change every-ting lak' a dead. Me no dead yet! A want it change back!"

"Daddy," Ma said, "that's not even important right now."

"You mean to tell me a gone a couple a days and you rearrange de whole ting like me naw come back. Kadeem is how you lay she do dis?" He looked at me.

I shrugged my shoulders. I knew better than to come between Ma and Grandad. No matter who's side I took, someone wouldn't be happy. Tess and her dad also remained silent.

The headmaster and Ma helped Grandad into his bed and got him settled. Me and Tess heard him fussing with them.

Grandad said, "I doan waan jus' lay here."

"Just tucking you in for a little bit, Daddy," said Ma.

"Me ain't you chile, eh," Ma closed that door and we couldn't hear them anymore.

It was just me and Tess alone in the kitchen now, the headmaster in Grandad's bedroom with Ma and Grandad. Although we couldn't hear them, I could imagine Grandad was not making it easy. He wasn't the type to just sit and let people take care of him, and this is what he was mostly fussing about.

"You tink you gon' gah tu go back?" Tess asked.

"What? What do you mean?" I hadn't thought ahead of getting Grandad out of the hospital, what his condition would be and what that might mean for me.

"A mean, you know," Tess fumbled with her words like she didn't really want to ask what she wanted to ask. "Because you gran-far-da doan seem able to tek care a you right now."

"I don't need taking care of, Tess," I blurted out, "I'm basically a grown man."

"Basically," Tess said doubtfully. "Dis why you gon need somebody who able, and right now you gran-far-da doan look like he able."

"She's right," Ma said. She and the headmaster came out of the bedroom. "You can't stay here, you and Daddy gonna have to go back with me; that's the only way I can do this!"

"Do what?" I shouted. If my skin were a lighter color, I was certain that everyone could see my skin turning red.

"Take care of you and Daddy both."

"You ain't been taking care me, Ma," I shouted, "we been fine, right here, without you."

"Calm dung, Kadeem," Tess suggested.

"No!" I shouted, "she can't just come here and change everything."

"Kadeem," Ma said calmly. Her voice always dropped when she was trying to convince me to do something. "It's just not feasible for you to stay here. Daddy is not at his best..."

"Who not at day best?" Grandad came out of the bedroom and joined us in the now crowded kitchen.

"Daddy," Ma shouted, "you should be in bed!"

"Gyal, I done tell you is me is de parent eh, not you," Grandad said as he tried to make his way to one of the seats in the kitchen. The headmaster helped and this time Grandad steadied on his arm without fanning his hand away. "Now, wa stru-pid-ness you out ya a talk bout?"

"She wants me to go back with her," I complained hoping that he could change her mind.

"Fuss' off, is who is *she*?"

"Ma, Grandad," I corrected, "Ma wants to take me back."

Tears welled up at the corner of my eyes threatening to show my anger and frustration.

"Doan go bawl dung de place, bwoy," Grandad said.

"Is okay, Kadeem." Tess stood closer to me and intertwined her fingers in mine.

"It's not okay." I yelled. "It's not, you can't just come here and all of a sudden change things. I like it here,"

"Fuss' off, Kadeem," Grandad looked up at me from his seat at the table, "lower you voice in ya."

"Yes, Grandad," I said.

"Gwendolyn, you cyan jus' come root up de chile lak' he a running vine, grow here, day, and every way." Grandad looked right at Ma when he spoke,

"But, Daddy..."

"*But, Daddy,* nut-un," Grandad pushed himself away from the table and tried to get up. Finally, he gave up. "Watch de bwoy. He look like he need or even want to go back?"

"No," Ma whispered.

"Egg-zack-ly," Grandad declared. That looked like it took a lot of energy from him to say that because his body sunk a little bit lower into the seat. "He naw go no way,"

Tess squeezed my hand. I had a choice here: float and go along with whatever the ocean brought or swim in the direction I chose. I knew that Ma loved me, you know, cause she had to. All mothers had to love their young, right? Except them animals that kill off their young right when they are born, but the others, like Ma, she had to love me. I knew now, though, that Grandad loved me too cause he was fighting to keep me here with him.

"Daddy, you're going to have to come with me. I won't be able to take care of you from Orlando, and I'm not leaving you here like this."

"Lak' wa?" Grandad asked. "Is tem-pa-rerry dis be, dis naw go lass for-ever. Me and Kadeem gon be fine."

"We are!" I declared.

"Plus, Lenwell naw go let nut-ton happen to us." Grandad looked at Tess' dad for confirmation, "right ,Lenwell?"

"Yes, of course," the headmaster agreed. "You'll be in good hands here!"

Ma gave him that death stare, that stare that she gave me when I was getting suspended, like she wanted to bury me where no one could find me ever again. The headmaster looked like he was sorry he'd said what he said, but the words had already left his mouth, and as much as he might like, he couldn't pack them back in.

"That's it den," Grandad pounded his hand on the table. He tried his best not to grimace, but his face betrayed him, sharing the pain that he really felt. "Me and Kadeem staying. Glad fa de visit, but is wa yo does say, Kadeem?"

"I don't know, Grandad, I say a lot of things."

"You know, dat ting."

"What thing?"

"We got dis!" Grandad shouted like he'd just discovered water in a dry desert land.

"Ok, Daddy," Ma submitted. It was like she finally got it. She finally understood that life was better for me here. This reality was the one that I wanted and needed. Here, like the ocean, possibilities didn't end.

We did it, we had it! Grandad and I were going to be fine. He was going to be playing soccer in no time, diving in no time, walking me home from school in no time, peeling sugar cane in no time. I'd found a home in the place and a person that I'd least expected.

Epilogue

December sometimes brought cold weather in Orlando, like that day when Ma wore her Uggs to work like she was going to a ski lodge. However, St. Kitts was still hot and the clothes people wore were evident of the heat. Their colorful costumes seemed like underwear cleverly decorated with an array of feathers for no birds that I knew of. Huge feathers, too big to be from a regular sized bird peeked between different colored paints and glitter to cover the rest of their bodies. Everyone in the crowd danced so closely that the squirming mass seemed joined together.

"Tess, do you ever dress like that?" I shouted over the loud music.

"Yeah, man," she laughed. "I does dance in de street in me panties, too but right now we got to play fa dis grade."

She was right. As much as I wanted to watch girls in panties parading through the streets, Tess was right. This was more important. With all the practicing we'd done, our only assessment for Band was playing during Carnival. Others gave tests throughout the school year, but the one shot we had to pass this class was Carnival. My part was easy, playing on the big drums. All I had to remember was when to hit one of the four parts of the drums. Tess had a lot of notes to remember. I didn't know how she managed, but she handled it like a real musician. We had more than one song too; there were several. Not only did we have to remember the notes, but we also had to play while standing on a moving long flatbed that was harnessed to a tractor. I wondered how I'd be able to balance while it moved. As for Tess, in true Tess fashion, she didn't seem worried at all.

We still stood in the street waiting to climb on top of the tractor. Made specifically for our school band, a banner with the letters CHS hung from the back of the trailer. We all wore our t-shirts that proclaimed *Crayon High School Brass Band* on their fronts and our uniform bottoms.

"You ready?" Tess asked.

"Yeah," I said.

We loaded onto the tractor, Tess in the very front because like she always said, she held the melody. I was in the very back. Once I found my spot, way in the very back with the other three bass players, I could see that Tess was set, stick in hands. The tractor pulled off with a jerking motion almost throwing me flat on my butt. Fortunately, I grabbed onto the edge of the drums to keep from falling. Tess looked back at me and gave me the thumbs up with a questioning look on her face. Was she sure I was gonna fall when the tractor took off? I raised my thumb to let her know I was good; I hadn't fallen; I was okay.

The melody started which meant it was time for me to hit the drums. I did. Tess' dad, Ma and Grandad danced to the beat as they followed behind the tractor with the rest of our fans. Though just the parents of students in the band, in my head, they were our fans. Ma took time off to come see me play in the band. She said it was something she had done in high school too and didn't want to miss my turn. I was glad she came.

While the music played, Grandad stopped for a moment, grabbed Ma's arm and twirled her around as though they were on the dance floor of *Dancing With the Stars*. Ma laughed. Grandad lifted his head toward me, signaling his approval.

Acknowledgment:

Thank you,
To my Ace,
Cheryl Race
For your continuous support
And encouragement.
I love that our lunches
End
With dinners!

About the Author

Leah T. Williams was born and raised in St. Kitts, a beautiful island in the West Indies. With her family, she resides in Central Florida where she teaches Language Arts to her sometimes-wonderful middle schoolers. Neither Out Far Nor In Deep is her first novel. Follow her on all Social Media outlets: Kittiwriter1.

Don't miss out!

Visit the website below and you can sign up to receive emails whenever Leah T. Williams publishes a new book. There's no charge and no obligation.

https://books2read.com/r/B-A-NKQW-MCWEC

BOOKS 2 READ

Connecting independent readers to independent writers.